GEORGE O'CONNOR

POSEIDON
EARTH SHAKER

A NEAL PORTER BOOK

First Second

New York

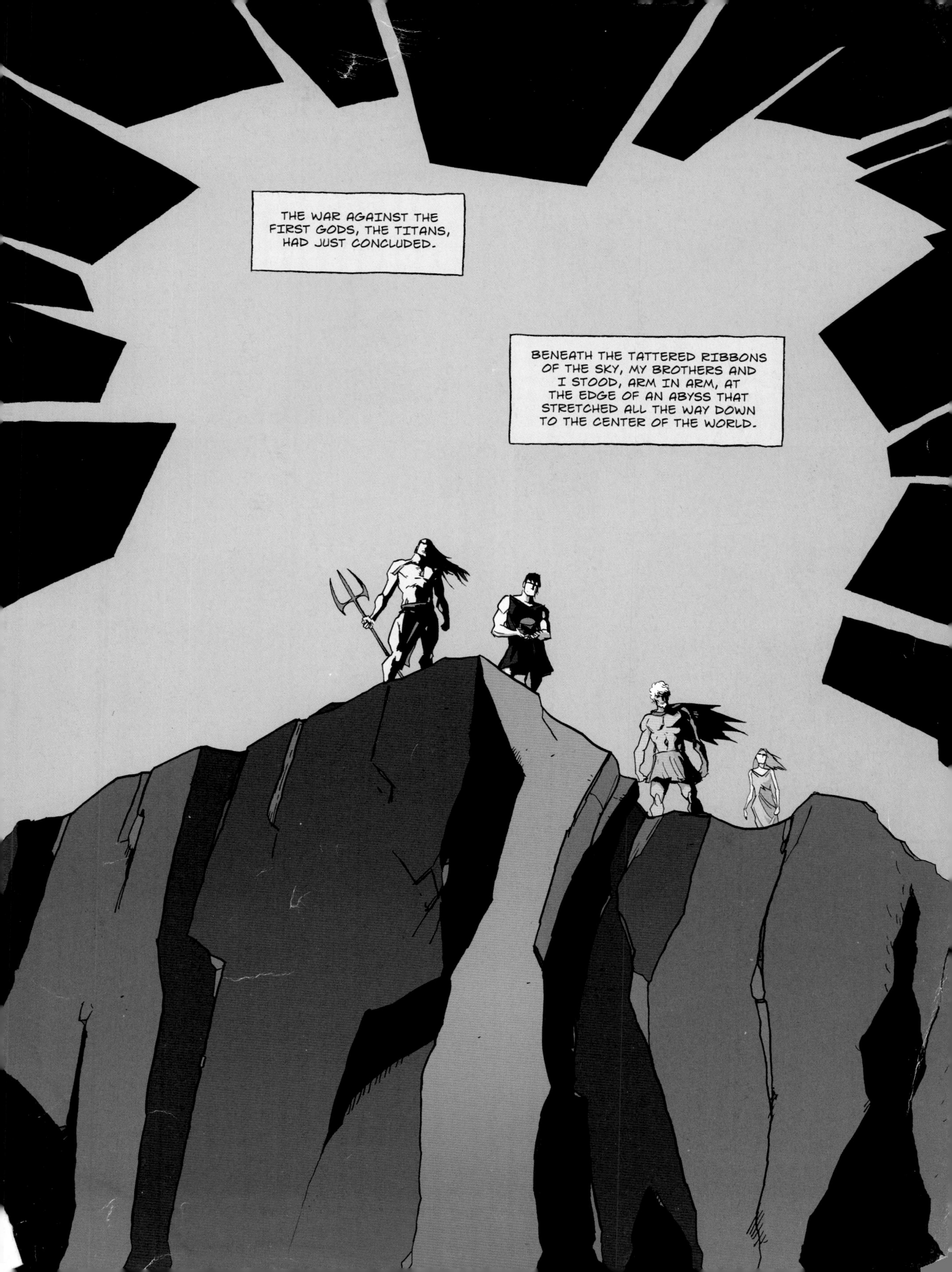
THE WAR AGAINST THE FIRST GODS, THE TITANS, HAD JUST CONCLUDED.
BENEATH THE TATTERED RIBBONS OF THE SKY, MY BROTHERS AND I STOOD, ARM IN ARM, AT THE EDGE OF AN ABYSS THAT STRETCHED ALL THE WAY DOWN TO THE CENTER OF THE WORLD.

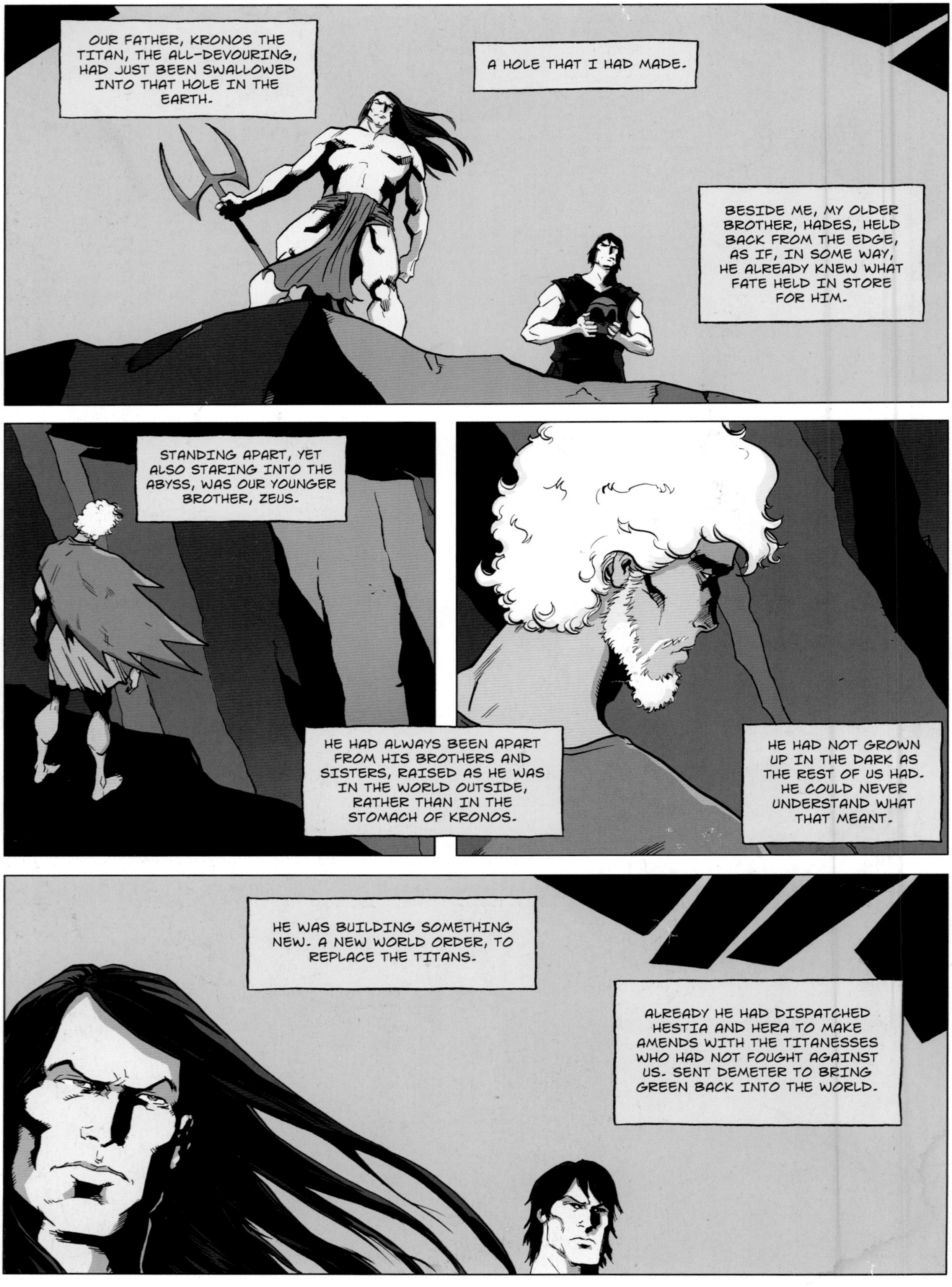
OUR FATHER, KRONOS THE TITAN, THE ALL-DEVOURING, HAD JUST BEEN SWALLOWED INTO THAT HOLE IN THE EARTH.
A HOLE THAT I HAD MADE.
BESIDE ME, MY OLDER BROTHER, HADES, HELD BACK FROM THE EDGE, AS IF, IN SOME WAY, HE ALREADY KNEW WHAT FATE HELD IN STORE FOR HIM.
STANDING APART, YET ALSO STARING INTO THE ABYSS, WAS OUR YOUNGER BROTHER, ZEUS.
HE HAD ALWAYS BEEN APART FROM HIS BROTHERS AND SISTERS, RAISED AS HE WAS IN THE WORLD OUTSIDE, RATHER THAN IN THE STOMACH OF KRONOS.
HE HAD NOT GROWN UP IN THE DARK AS THE REST OF US HAD. HE COULD NEVER UNDERSTAND WHAT THAT MEANT.
HE WAS BUILDING SOMETHING NEW. A NEW WORLD ORDER, TO REPLACE THE TITANS.
ALREADY HE HAD DISPATCHED HESTIA AND HERA TO MAKE AMENDS WITH THE TITANESSES WHO HAD NOT FOUGHT AGAINST US. SENT DEMETER TO BRING GREEN BACK INTO THE WORLD.

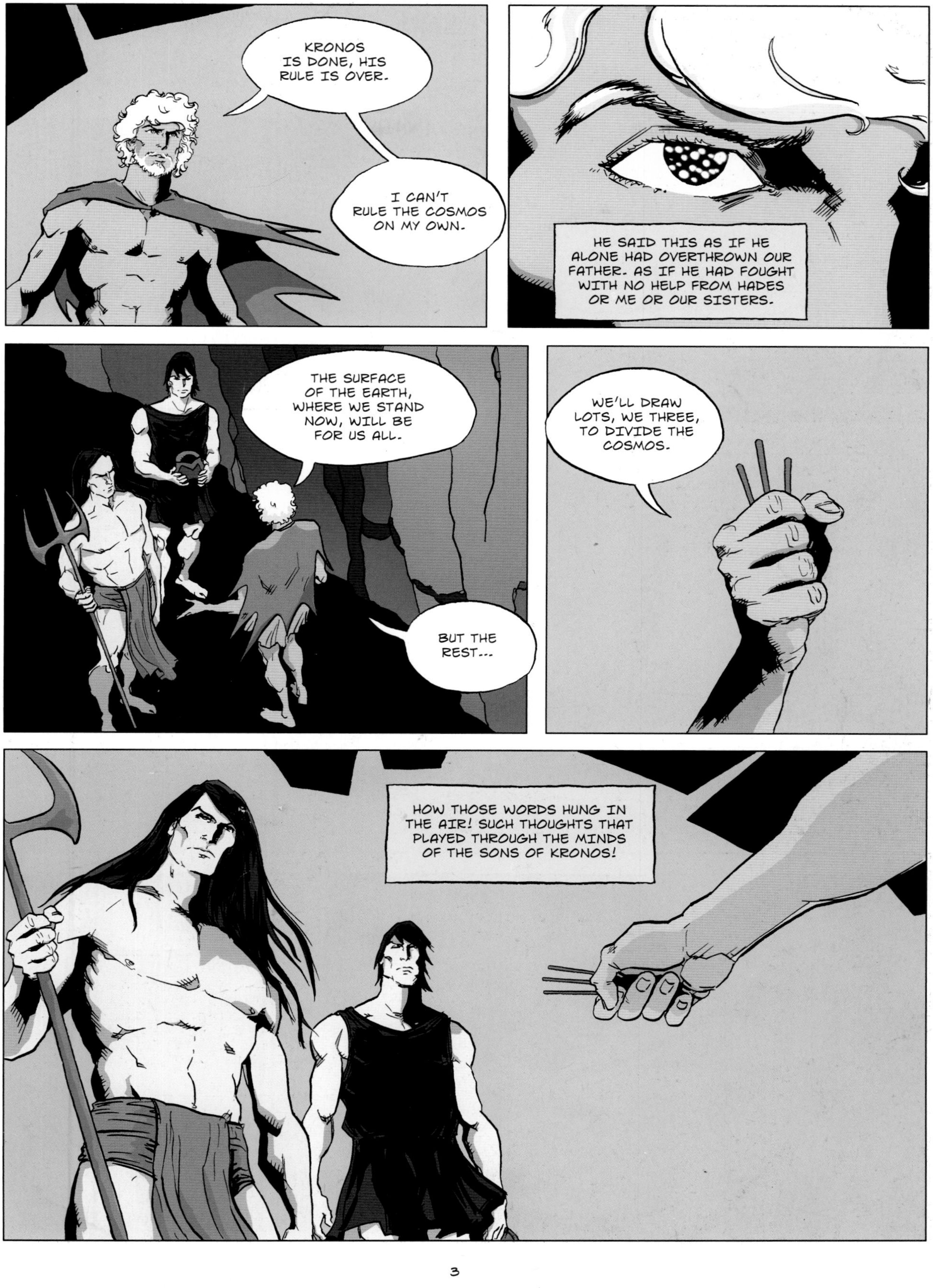
KRONOS IS DONE, HIS RULE IS OVER.
I CAN'T RULE THE COSMOS ON MY OWN.
HE SAID THIS AS IF HE ALONE HAD OVERTHROWN OUR FATHER. AS IF HE HAD FOUGHT WITH NO HELP FROM HADES OR ME OR OUR SISTERS.
THE SURFACE OF THE EARTH, WHERE WE STAND NOW, WILL BE FOR US ALL.
BUT THE REST...
WE'LL DRAW LOTS, WE THREE, TO DIVIDE THE COSMOS.
HOW THOSE WORDS HUNG IN THE AIR! SUCH THOUGHTS THAT PLAYED THROUGH THE MINDS OF THE SONS OF KRONOS!

HADES, THE ELDEST, DREW FIRST. HE HAD SPENT THE LONGEST TIME IN THE DARKNESS.

IT WAS THEREFORE FITTING, PERHAPS, THAT HE WAS AWARDED THE UNDERWORLD.

IF HE WAS DISAPPOINTED IN HIS ALLOTMENT, HE GAVE NO SIGN. HIS TIME HIDDEN FROM SIGHT MADE HIM HARD TO READ.

ZEUS WAS AWARDED THE SKY. HE ALONE OF US GREW UP KNOWING IT, STARING INTO IT, AT THE SUN, THE MOON. THERE COULD BE NO OTHER WAY.

HE MADE HIS HOME ON THE TALLEST MOUNTAIN LEFT STANDING, CALLED OLYMPUS. HIS PALACE THRUST AS HIGH INTO THE CLOUDS AS IT COULD WHILE STILL TOUCHING THE EARTH.

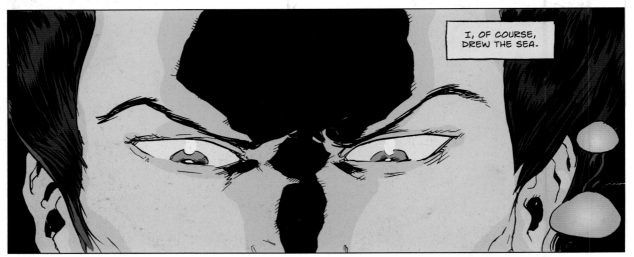

I, OF COURSE, DREW THE SEA.

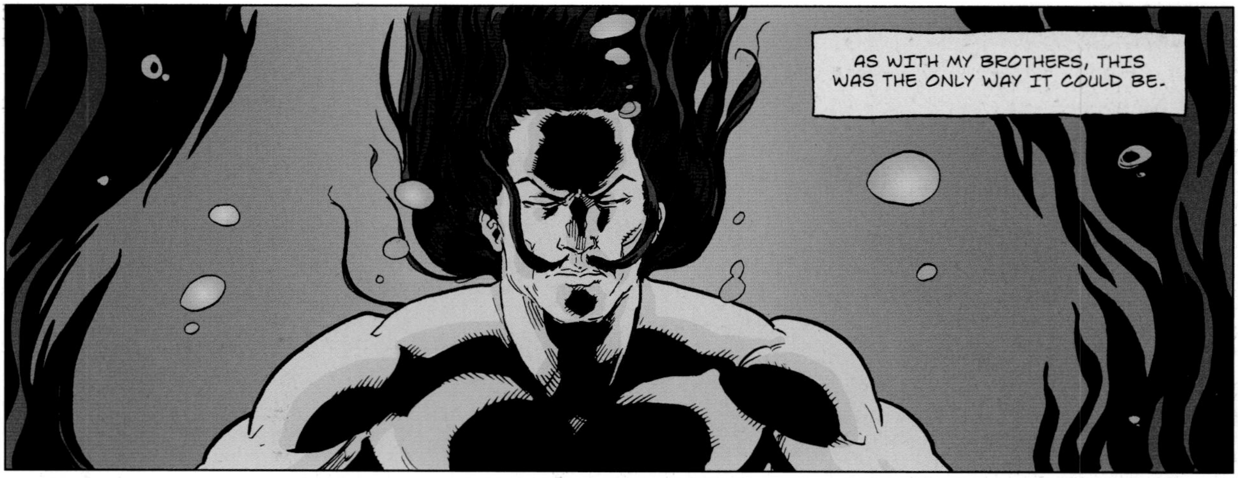
AS WITH MY BROTHERS, THIS
WAS THE ONLY WAY IT COULD BE.

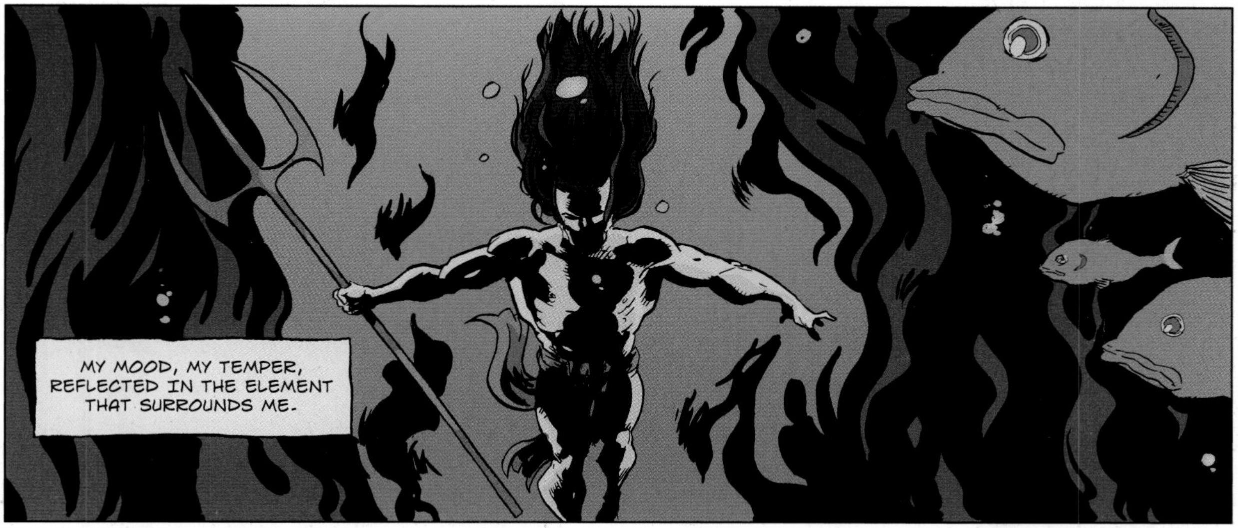
MY MOOD, MY TEMPER,
REFLECTED IN THE ELEMENT
THAT SURROUNDS ME.

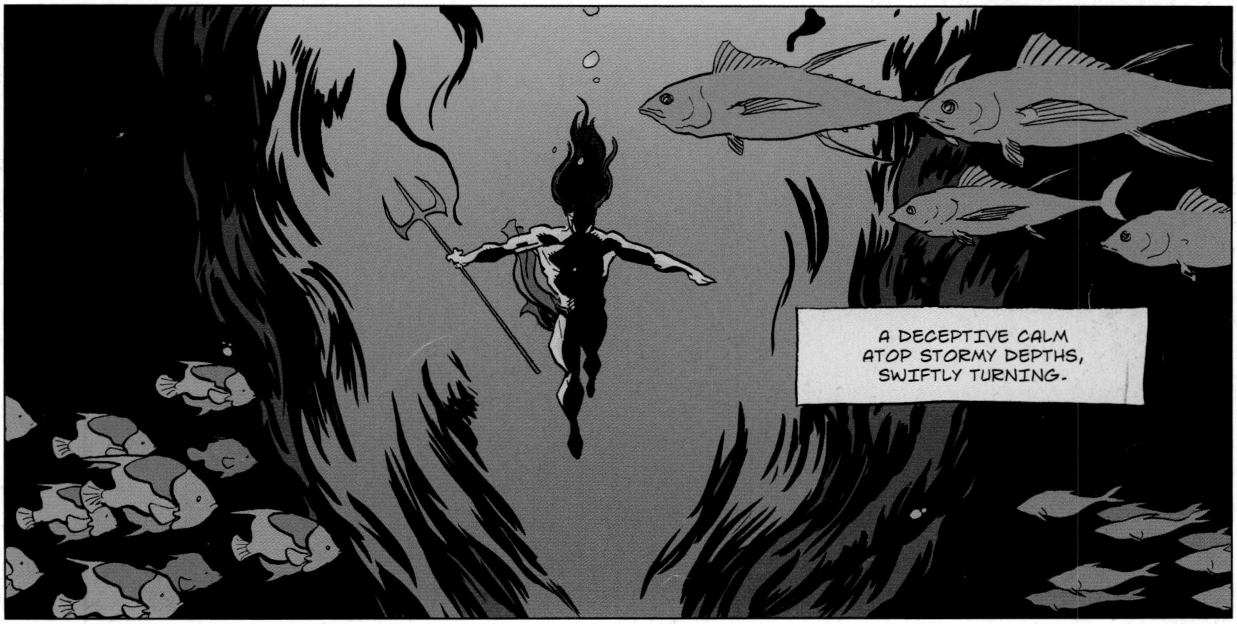
A DECEPTIVE CALM
ATOP STORMY DEPTHS,
SWIFTLY TURNING.

FROM THE BOTTOM OF THE DEEP GREEN-BLUE, MY ARMS REACH OUT ACROSS THE GLOBE AND HOLD IT IN EMBRACE.

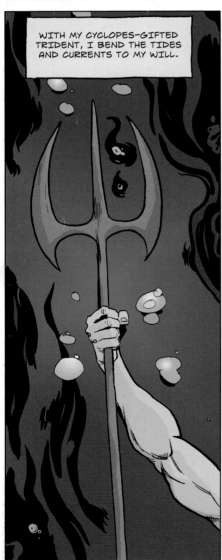

WITH MY CYCLOPES-GIFTED TRIDENT, I BEND THE TIDES AND CURRENTS TO MY WILL.

THE WAVES SLIDE FROM MY DARK HAIR.

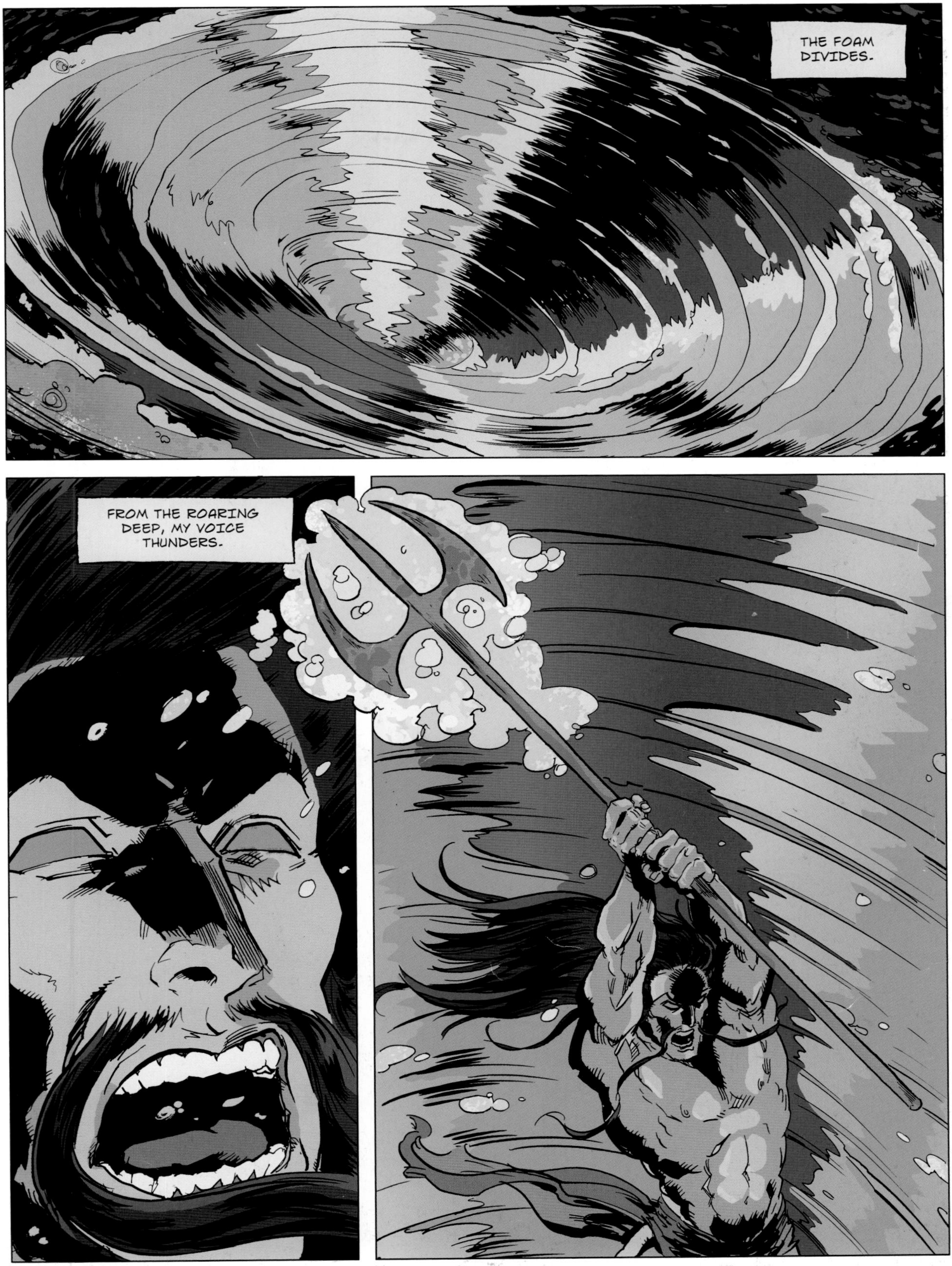
THE FOAM DIVIDES.
FROM THE ROARING DEEP, MY VOICE THUNDERS.

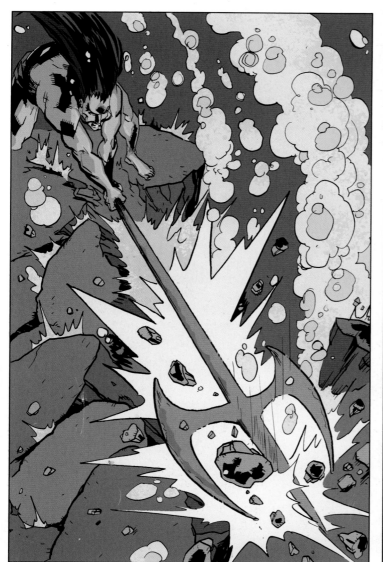

THE SEA BOILS FIERCELY.

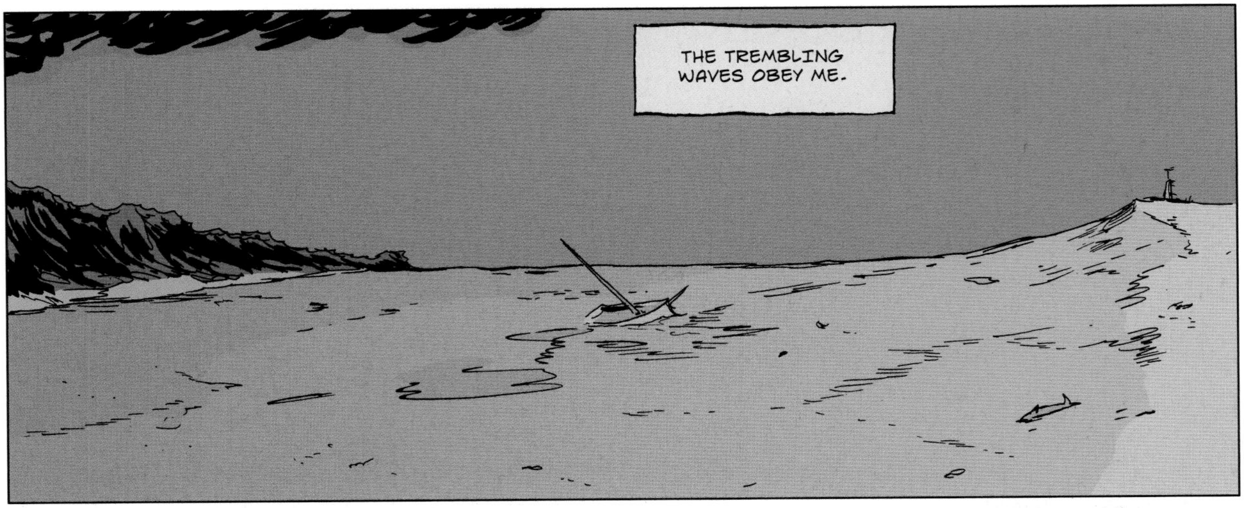
THE TREMBLING WAVES OBEY ME.

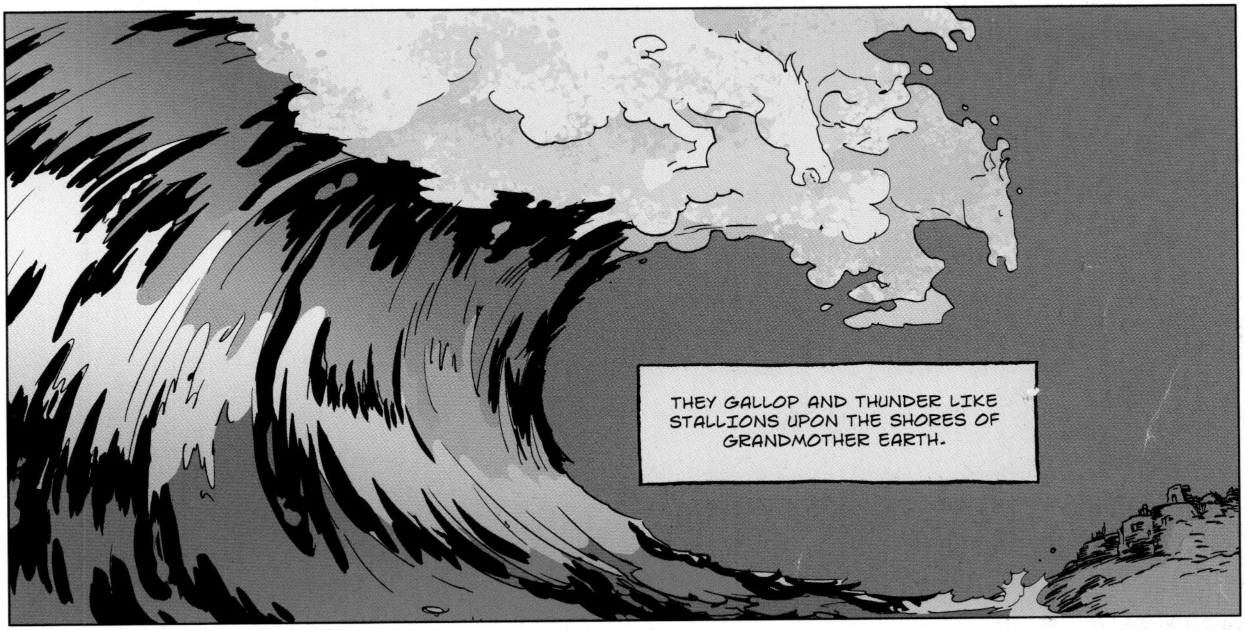
THEY GALLOP AND THUNDER LIKE STALLIONS UPON THE SHORES OF GRANDMOTHER EARTH.

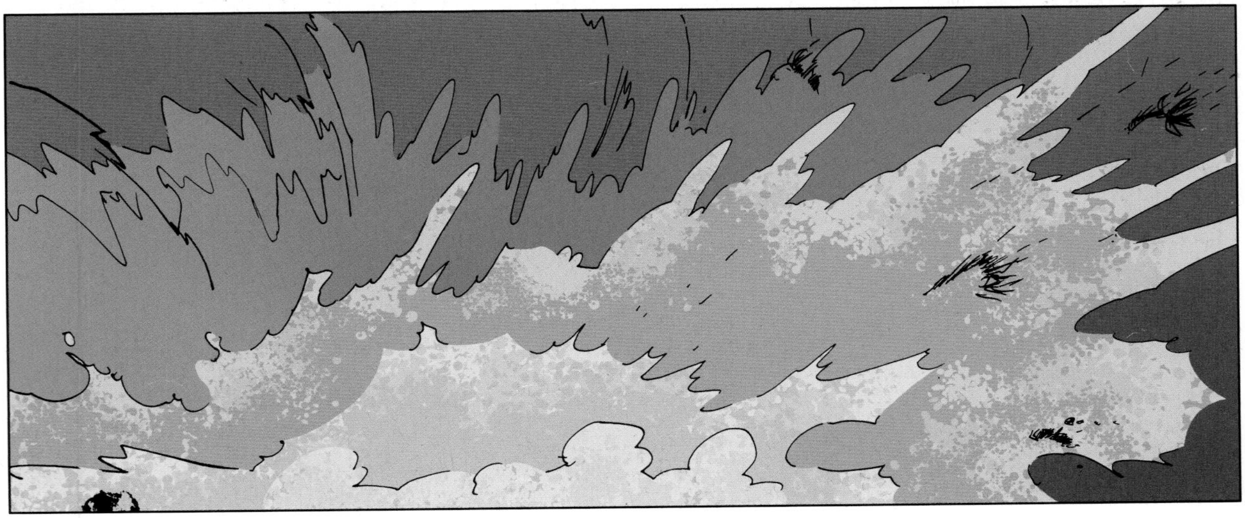

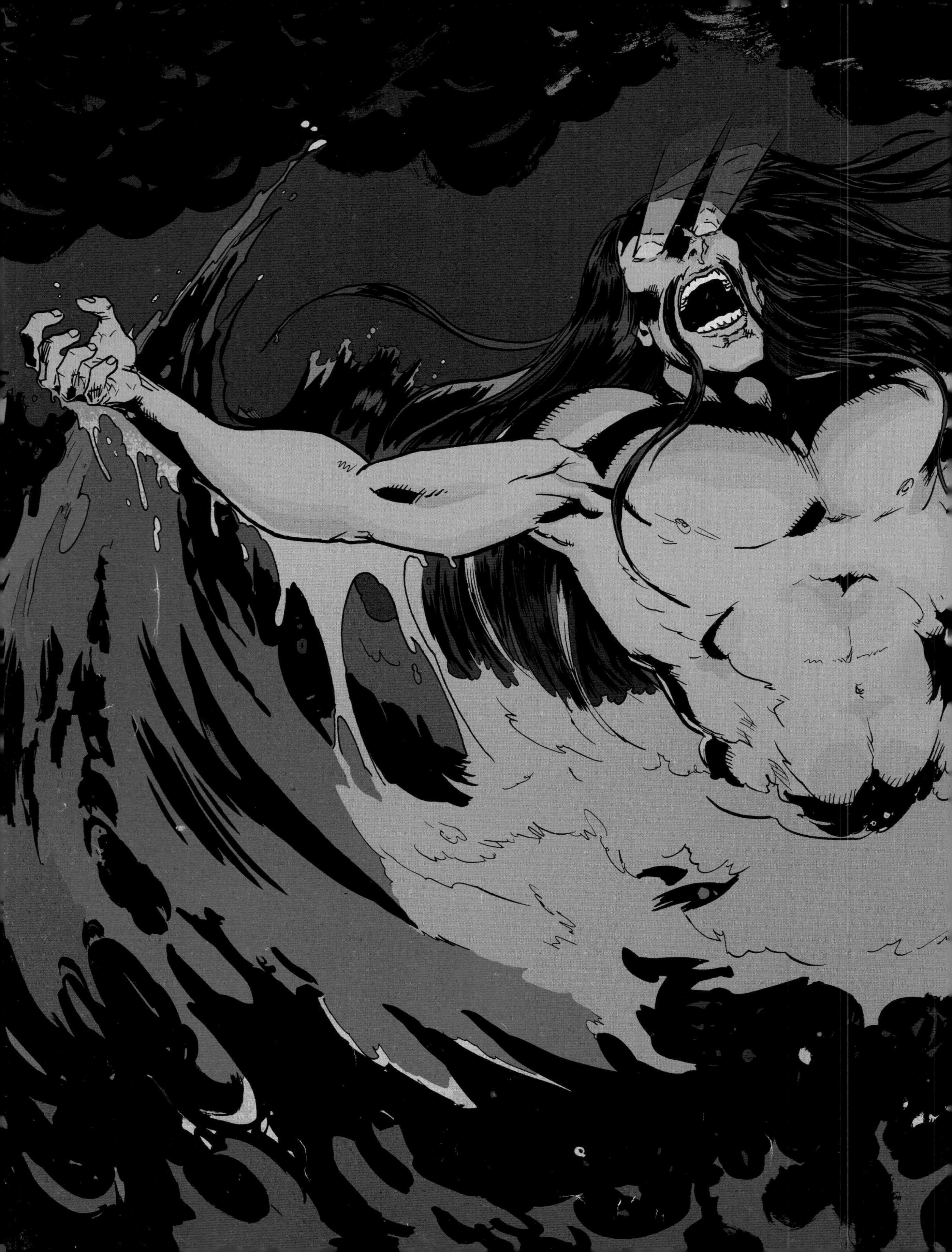

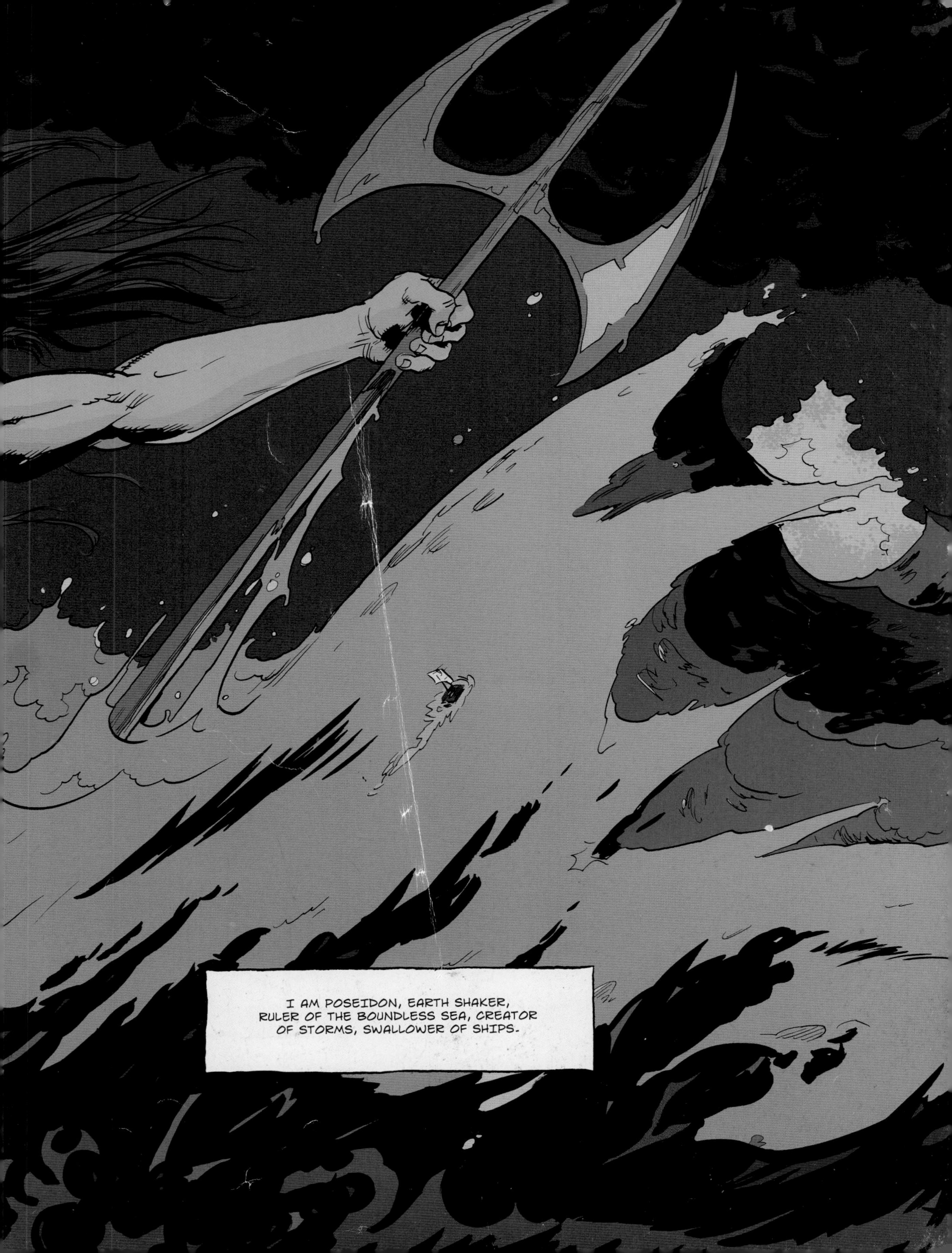
I AM POSEIDON, EARTH SHAKER, RULER OF THE BOUNDLESS SEA, CREATOR OF STORMS, SWALLOWER OF SHIPS.

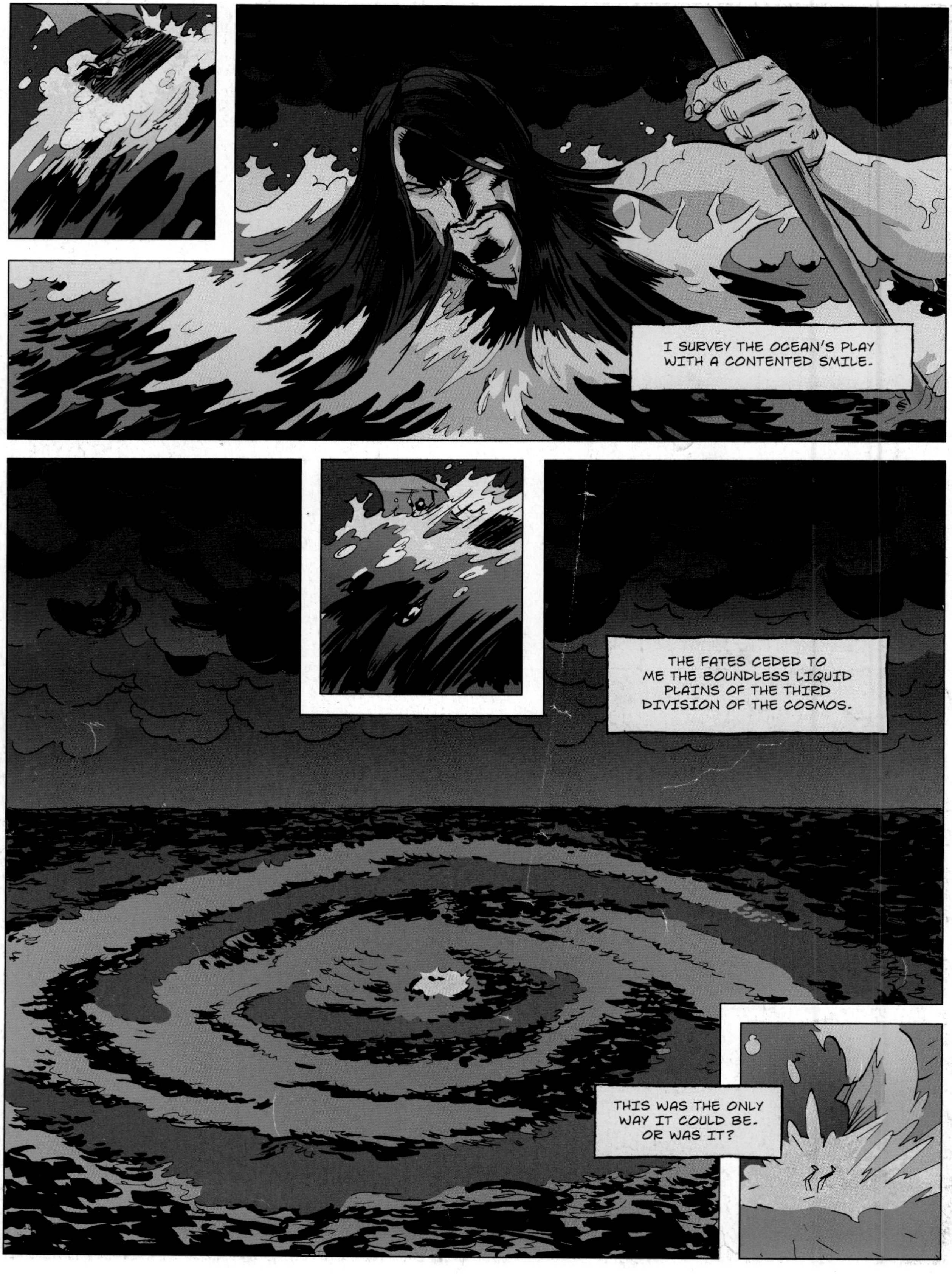
I SURVEY THE OCEAN'S PLAY WITH A CONTENTED SMILE.
THE FATES CEDED TO ME THE BOUNDLESS LIQUID PLAINS OF THE THIRD DIVISION OF THE COSMOS.
THIS WAS THE ONLY WAY IT COULD BE. OR WAS IT?

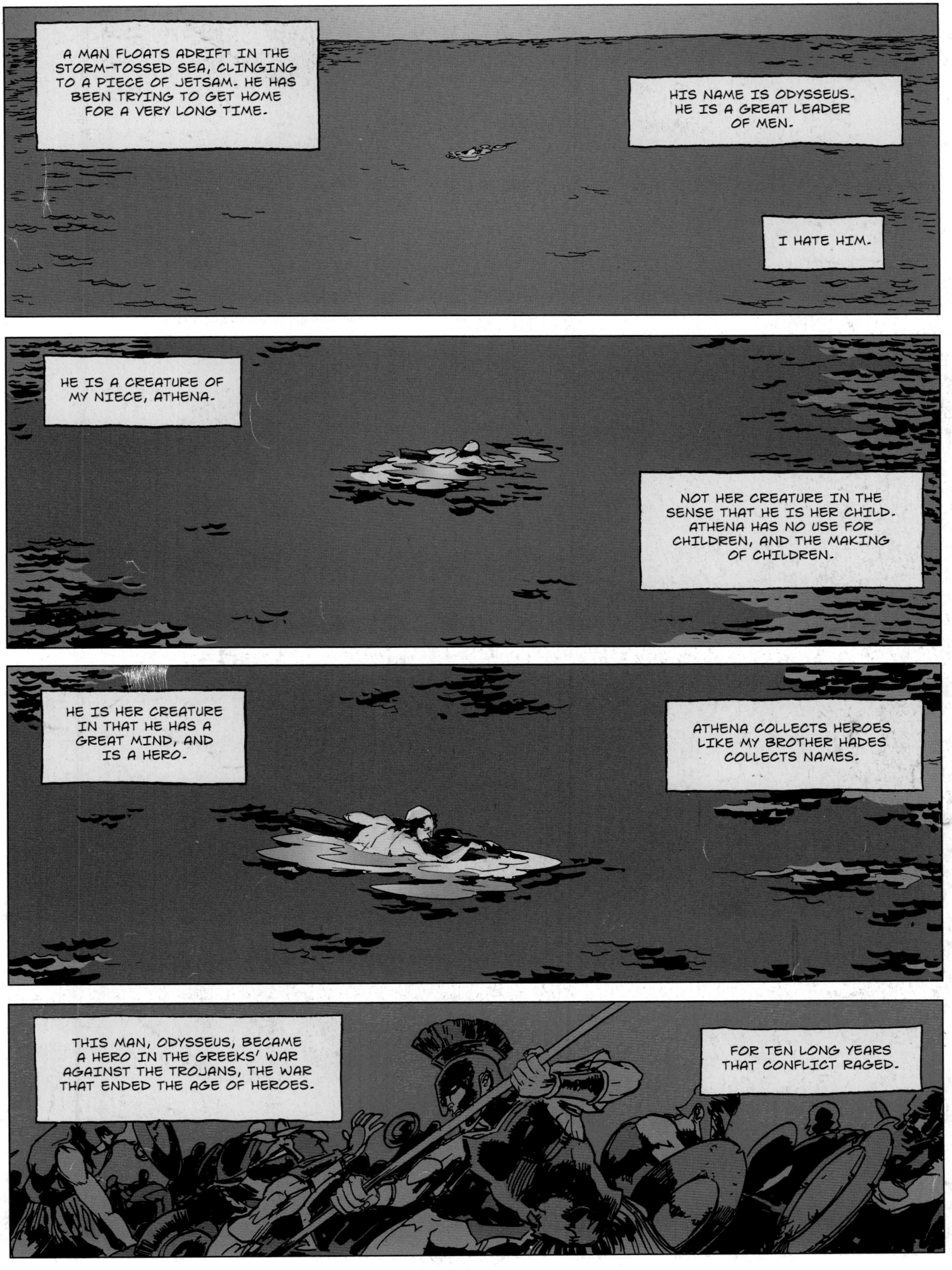
A MAN FLOATS ADRIFT IN THE STORM-TOSSED SEA, CLINGING TO A PIECE OF JETSAM. HE HAS BEEN TRYING TO GET HOME FOR A VERY LONG TIME.
HIS NAME IS ODYSSEUS. HE IS A GREAT LEADER OF MEN.
I HATE HIM.
HE IS A CREATURE OF MY NIECE, ATHENA.
NOT HER CREATURE IN THE SENSE THAT HE IS HER CHILD. ATHENA HAS NO USE FOR CHILDREN, AND THE MAKING OF CHILDREN.
HE IS HER CREATURE IN THAT HE HAS A GREAT MIND, AND IS A HERO.
ATHENA COLLECTS HEROES LIKE MY BROTHER HADES COLLECTS NAMES.
THIS MAN, ODYSSEUS, BECAME A HERO IN THE GREEKS' WAR AGAINST THE TROJANS, THE WAR THAT ENDED THE AGE OF HEROES.
FOR TEN LONG YEARS THAT CONFLICT RAGED.

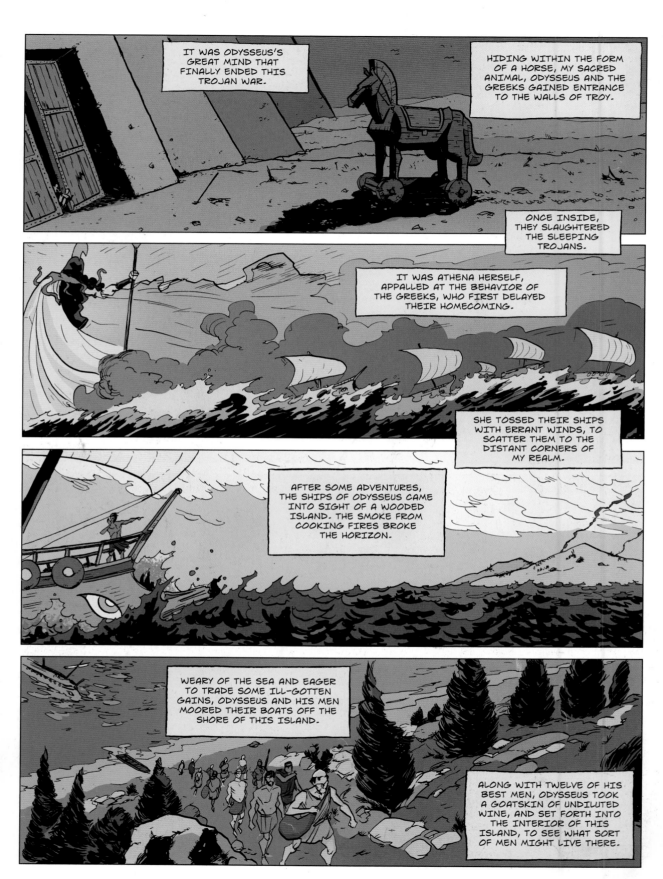

IT WAS ODYSSEUS'S GREAT MIND THAT FINALLY ENDED THIS TROJAN WAR.

HIDING WITHIN THE FORM OF A HORSE, MY SACRED ANIMAL, ODYSSEUS AND THE GREEKS GAINED ENTRANCE TO THE WALLS OF TROY.

ONCE INSIDE, THEY SLAUGHTERED THE SLEEPING TROJANS.

IT WAS ATHENA HERSELF, APPALLED AT THE BEHAVIOR OF THE GREEKS, WHO FIRST DELAYED THEIR HOMECOMING.

SHE TOSSED THEIR SHIPS WITH ERRANT WINDS, TO SCATTER THEM TO THE DISTANT CORNERS OF MY REALM.

AFTER SOME ADVENTURES, THE SHIPS OF ODYSSEUS CAME INTO SIGHT OF A WOODED ISLAND. THE SMOKE FROM COOKING FIRES BROKE THE HORIZON.

WEARY OF THE SEA AND EAGER TO TRADE SOME ILL-GOTTEN GAINS, ODYSSEUS AND HIS MEN MOORED THEIR BOATS OFF THE SHORE OF THIS ISLAND.

ALONG WITH TWELVE OF HIS BEST MEN, ODYSSEUS TOOK A GOATSKIN OF UNDILUTED WINE, AND SET FORTH INTO THE INTERIOR OF THIS ISLAND, TO SEE WHAT SORT OF MEN MIGHT LIVE THERE.

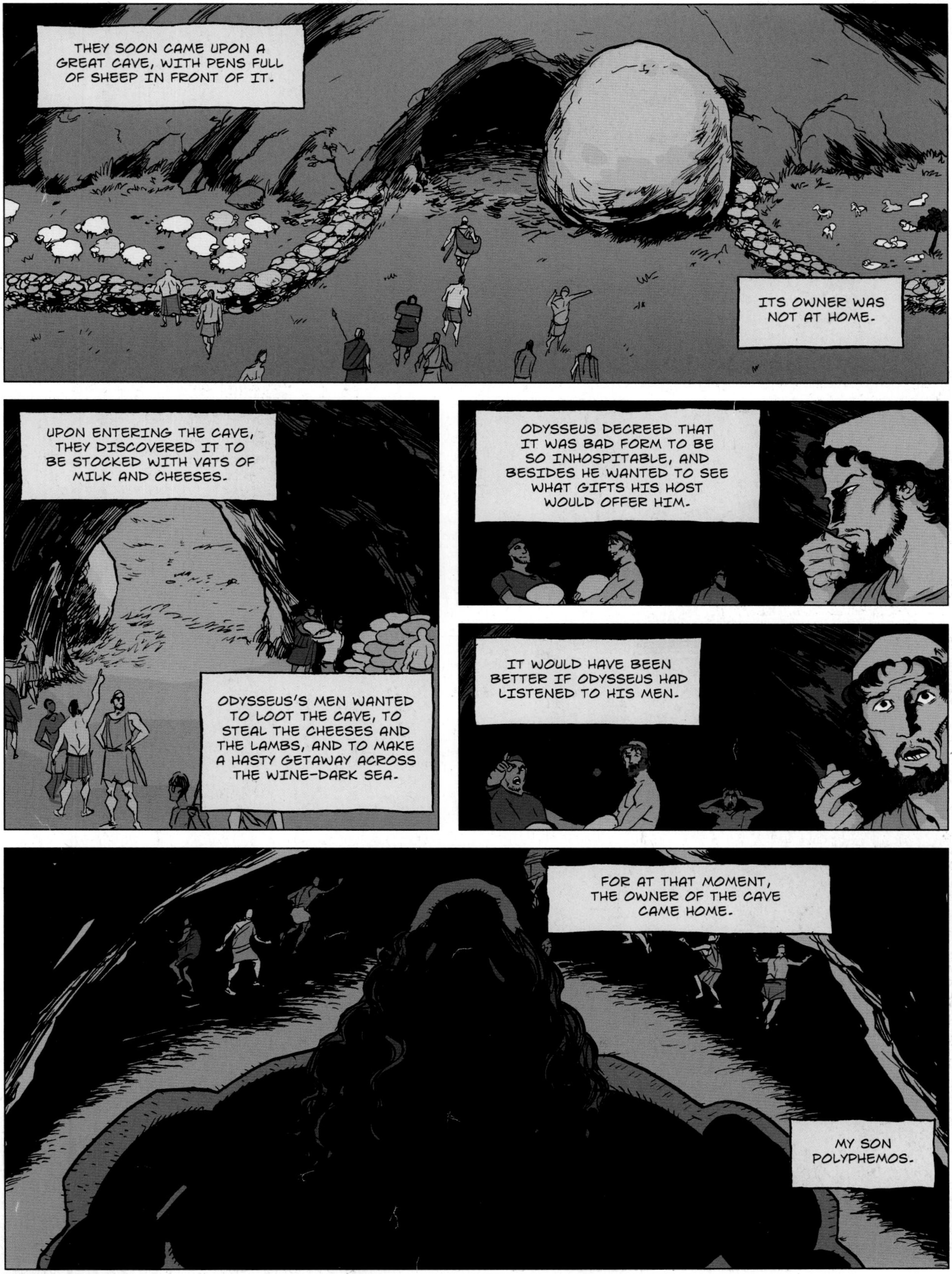
THEY SOON CAME UPON A GREAT CAVE, WITH PENS FULL OF SHEEP IN FRONT OF IT.
ITS OWNER WAS NOT AT HOME.
UPON ENTERING THE CAVE, THEY DISCOVERED IT TO BE STOCKED WITH VATS OF MILK AND CHEESES.
ODYSSEUS'S MEN WANTED TO LOOT THE CAVE, TO STEAL THE CHEESES AND THE LAMBS, AND TO MAKE A HASTY GETAWAY ACROSS THE WINE-DARK SEA.
ODYSSEUS DECREED THAT IT WAS BAD FORM TO BE SO INHOSPITABLE, AND BESIDES HE WANTED TO SEE WHAT GIFTS HIS HOST WOULD OFFER HIM.
IT WOULD HAVE BEEN BETTER IF ODYSSEUS HAD LISTENED TO HIS MEN.
FOR AT THAT MOMENT, THE OWNER OF THE CAVE CAME HOME.
MY SON POLYPHEMOS.

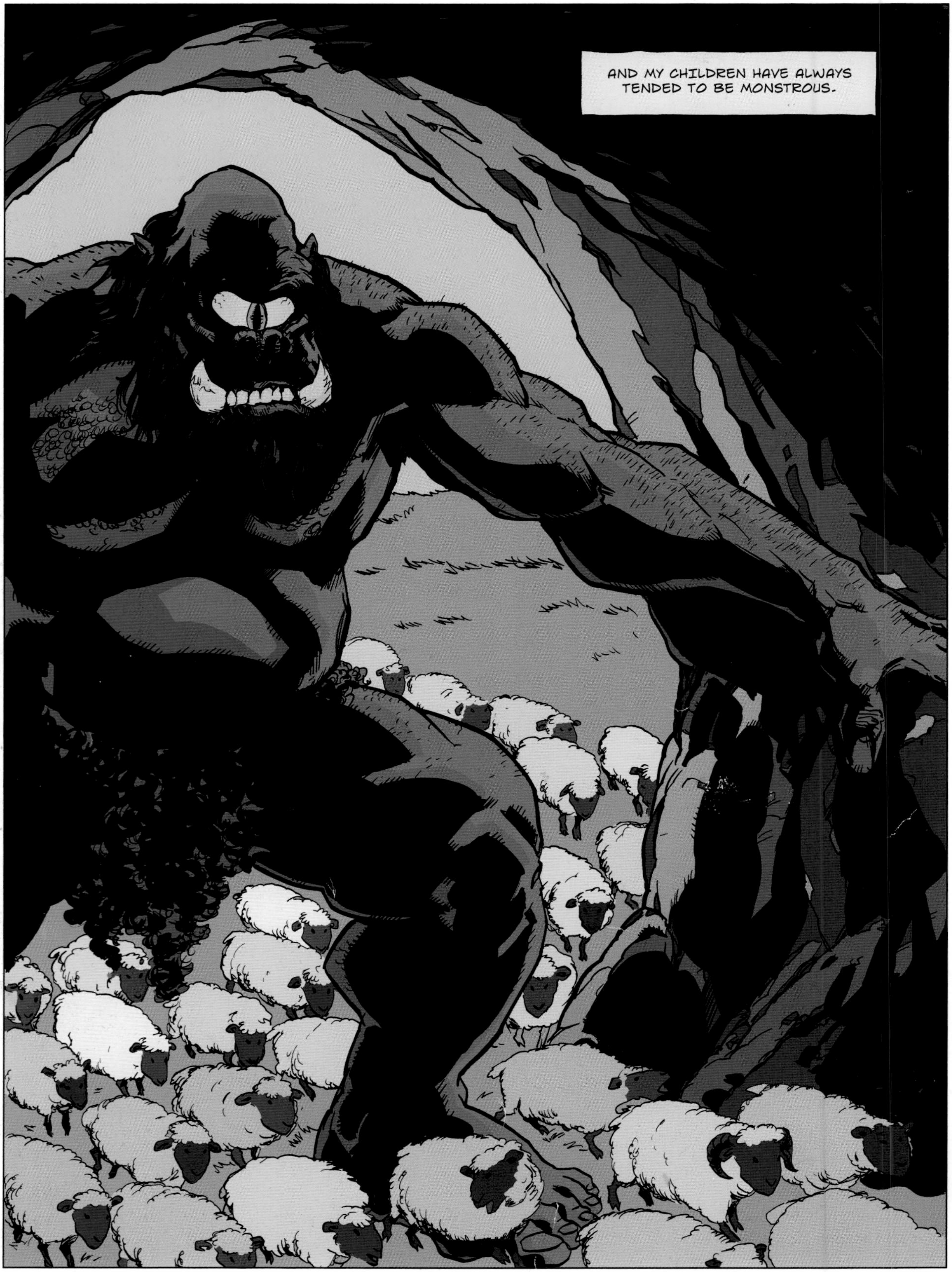
AND MY CHILDREN HAVE ALWAYS TENDED TO BE MONSTROUS.

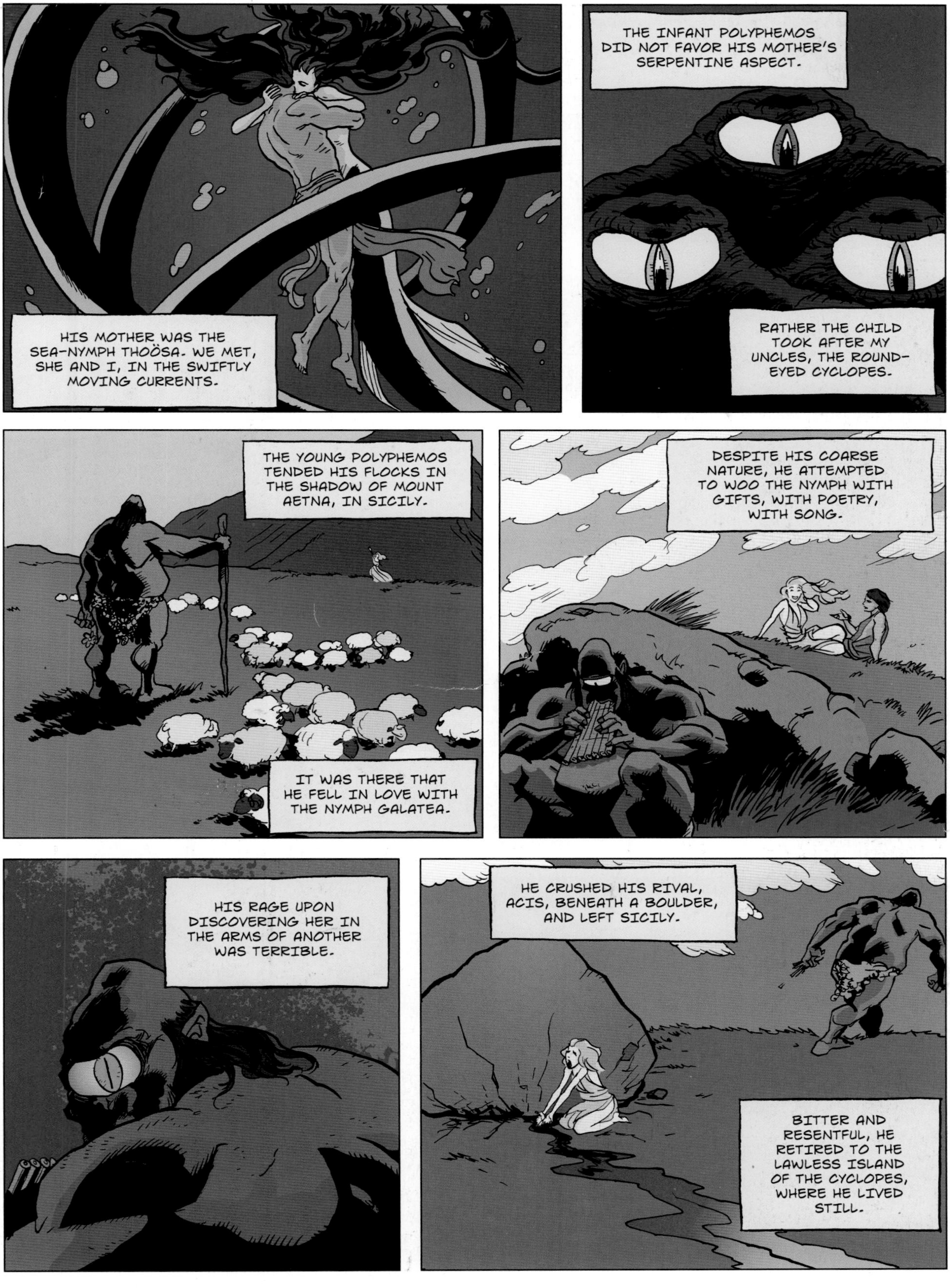
HIS MOTHER WAS THE SEA-NYMPH THOÖSA. WE MET, SHE AND I, IN THE SWIFTLY MOVING CURRENTS.
THE INFANT POLYPHEMOS DID NOT FAVOR HIS MOTHER'S SERPENTINE ASPECT.
RATHER THE CHILD TOOK AFTER MY UNCLES, THE ROUND-EYED CYCLOPES.
THE YOUNG POLYPHEMOS TENDED HIS FLOCKS IN THE SHADOW OF MOUNT AETNA, IN SICILY.
IT WAS THERE THAT HE FELL IN LOVE WITH THE NYMPH GALATEA.
DESPITE HIS COARSE NATURE, HE ATTEMPTED TO WOO THE NYMPH WITH GIFTS, WITH POETRY, WITH SONG.
HIS RAGE UPON DISCOVERING HER IN THE ARMS OF ANOTHER WAS TERRIBLE.
HE CRUSHED HIS RIVAL, ACIS, BENEATH A BOULDER, AND LEFT SICILY.
BITTER AND RESENTFUL, HE RETIRED TO THE LAWLESS ISLAND OF THE CYCLOPES, WHERE HE LIVED STILL.

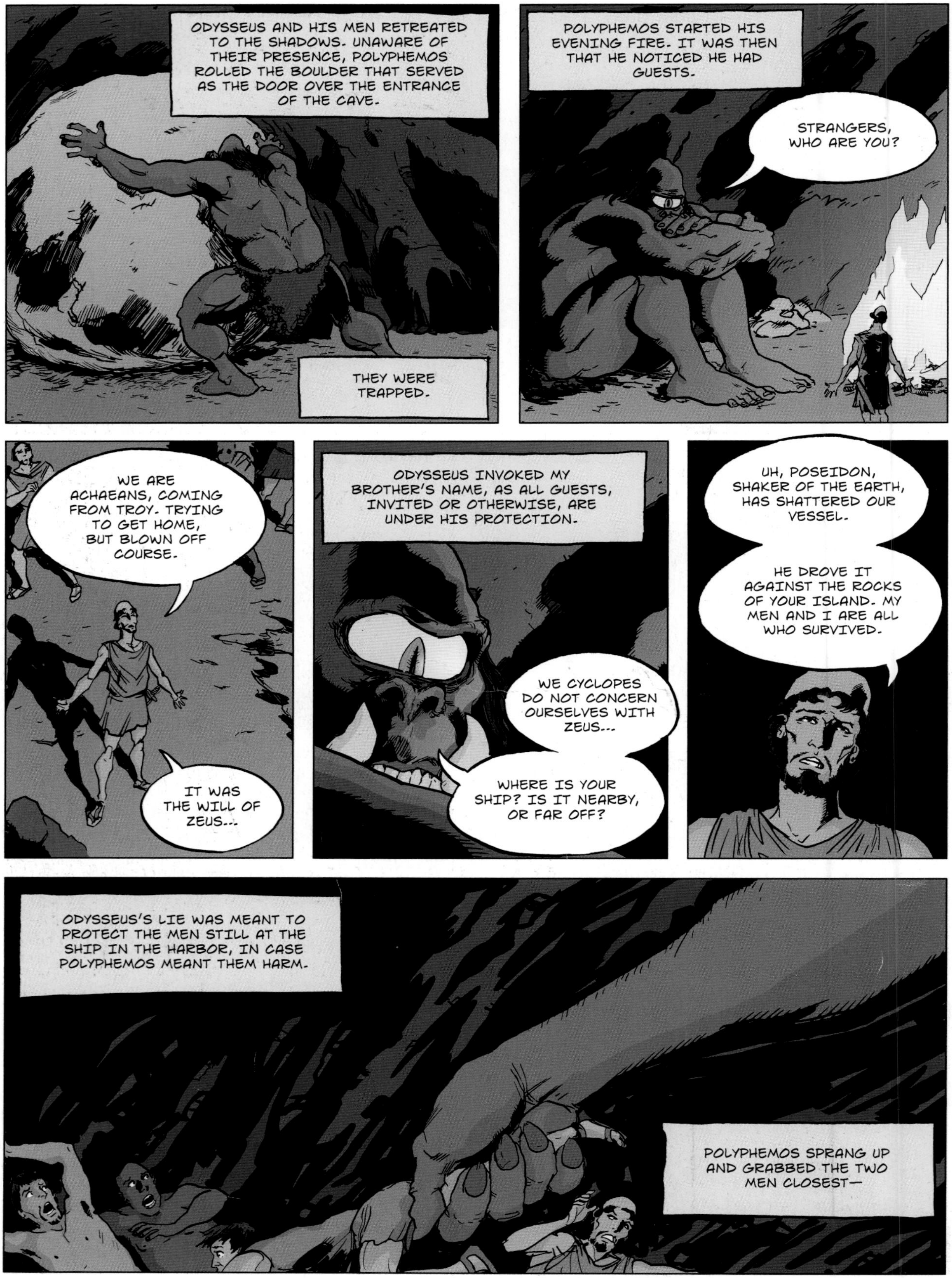
ODYSSEUS AND HIS MEN RETREATED TO THE SHADOWS. UNAWARE OF THEIR PRESENCE, POLYPHEMOS ROLLED THE BOULDER THAT SERVED AS THE DOOR OVER THE ENTRANCE OF THE CAVE.
THEY WERE TRAPPED.
POLYPHEMOS STARTED HIS EVENING FIRE. IT WAS THEN THAT HE NOTICED HE HAD GUESTS.
STRANGERS, WHO ARE YOU?
WE ARE ACHAEANS, COMING FROM TROY. TRYING TO GET HOME, BUT BLOWN OFF COURSE.
IT WAS THE WILL OF ZEUS...
ODYSSEUS INVOKED MY BROTHER'S NAME, AS ALL GUESTS, INVITED OR OTHERWISE, ARE UNDER HIS PROTECTION.
WE CYCLOPES DO NOT CONCERN OURSELVES WITH ZEUS...
WHERE IS YOUR SHIP? IS IT NEARBY, OR FAR OFF?
UH, POSEIDON, SHAKER OF THE EARTH, HAS SHATTERED OUR VESSEL.
HE DROVE IT AGAINST THE ROCKS OF YOUR ISLAND. MY MEN AND I ARE ALL WHO SURVIVED.
ODYSSEUS'S LIE WAS MEANT TO PROTECT THE MEN STILL AT THE SHIP IN THE HARBOR, IN CASE POLYPHEMOS MEANT THEM HARM.
POLYPHEMOS SPRANG UP AND GRABBED THE TWO MEN CLOSEST—

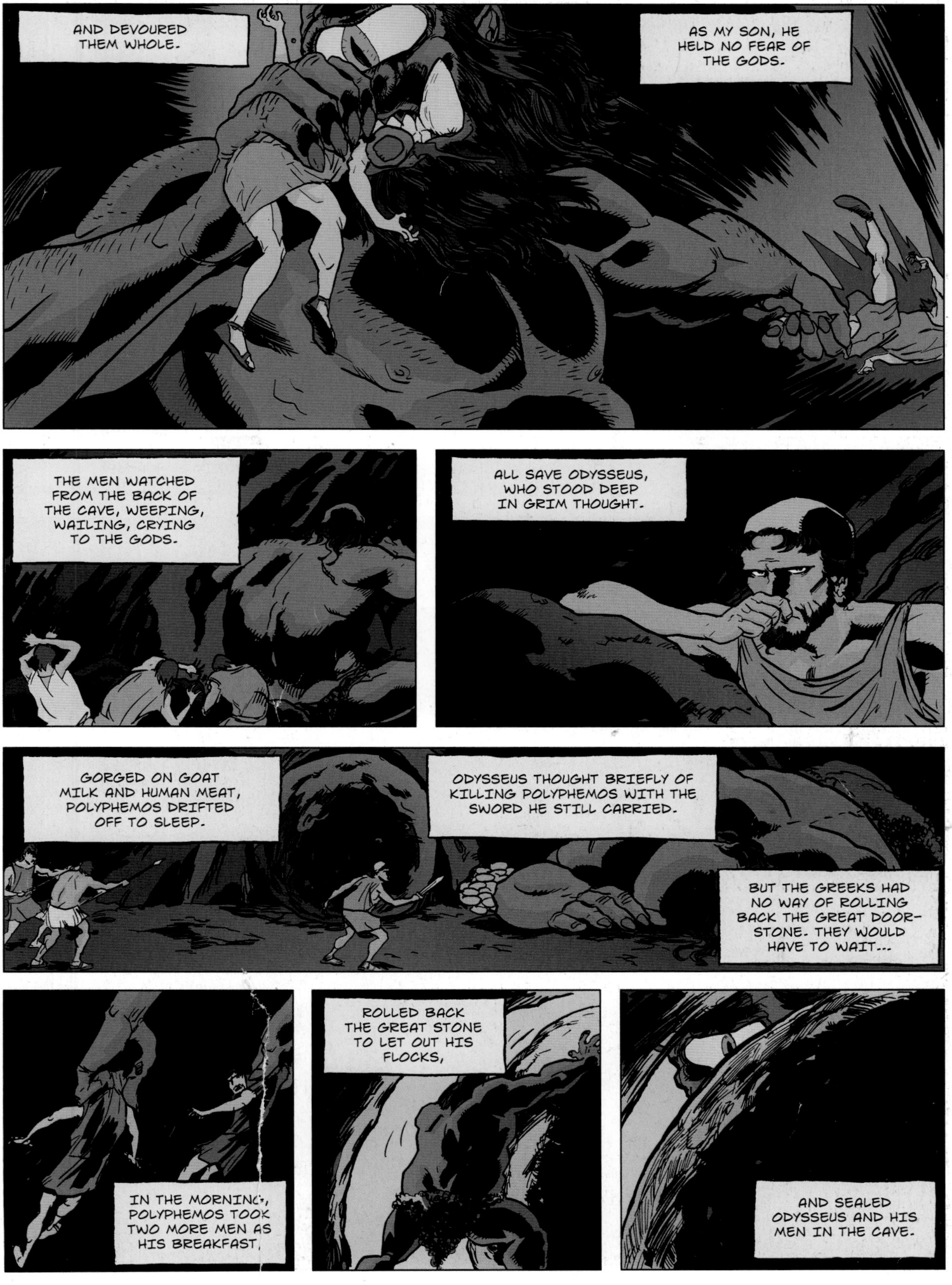
AND DEVOURED THEM WHOLE.
AS MY SON, HE HELD NO FEAR OF THE GODS.
THE MEN WATCHED FROM THE BACK OF THE CAVE, WEEPING, WAILING, CRYING TO THE GODS.
ALL SAVE ODYSSEUS, WHO STOOD DEEP IN GRIM THOUGHT.
GORGED ON GOAT MILK AND HUMAN MEAT, POLYPHEMOS DRIFTED OFF TO SLEEP.
ODYSSEUS THOUGHT BRIEFLY OF KILLING POLYPHEMOS WITH THE SWORD HE STILL CARRIED.
BUT THE GREEKS HAD NO WAY OF ROLLING BACK THE GREAT DOOR-STONE. THEY WOULD HAVE TO WAIT...
IN THE MORNING, POLYPHEMOS TOOK TWO MORE MEN AS HIS BREAKFAST,
ROLLED BACK THE GREAT STONE TO LET OUT HIS FLOCKS,
AND SEALED ODYSSEUS AND HIS MEN IN THE CAVE.

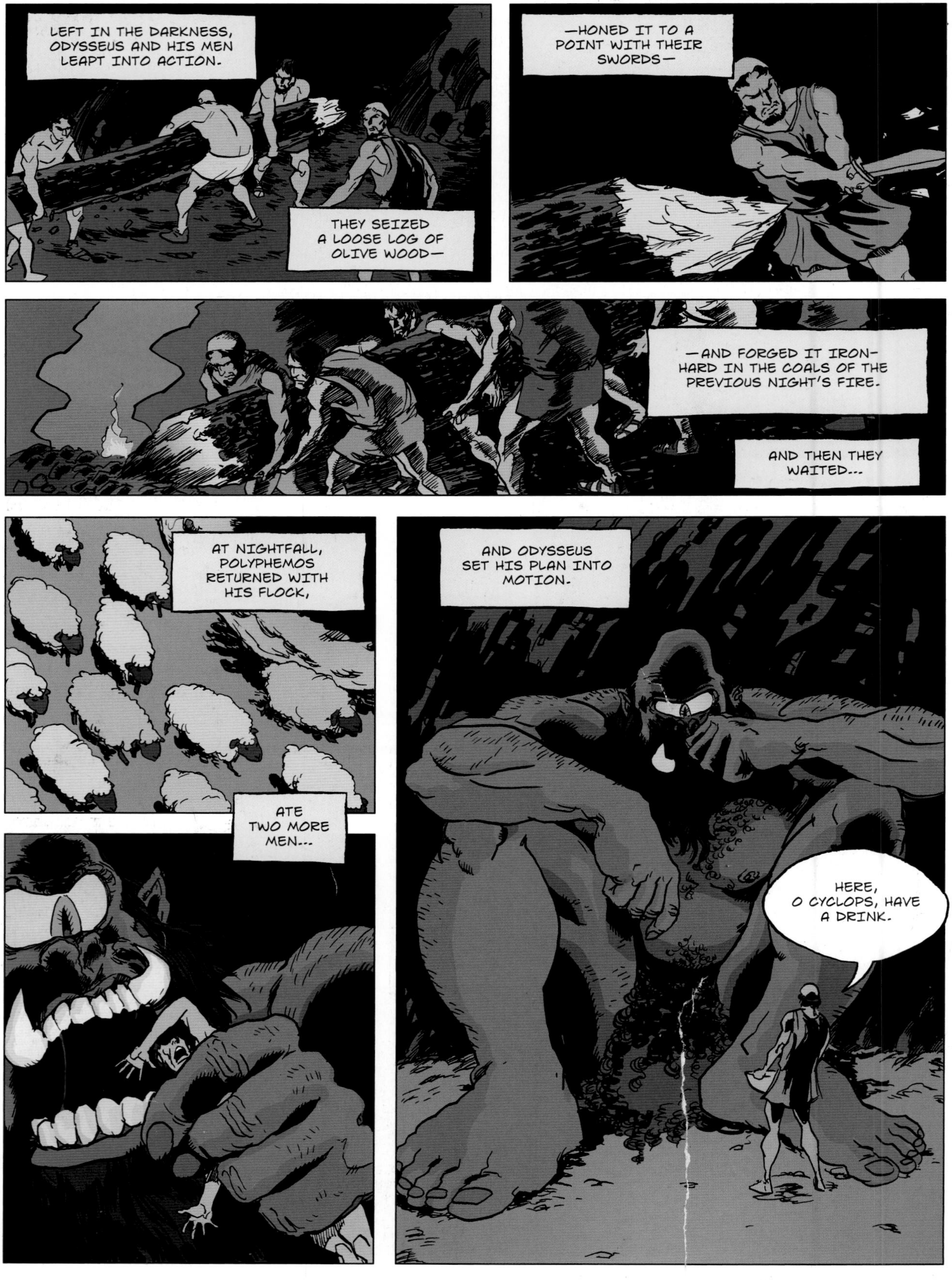
LEFT IN THE DARKNESS, ODYSSEUS AND HIS MEN LEAPT INTO ACTION.
THEY SEIZED A LOOSE LOG OF OLIVE WOOD—
—HONED IT TO A POINT WITH THEIR SWORDS—
—AND FORGED IT IRON-HARD IN THE COALS OF THE PREVIOUS NIGHT'S FIRE.
AND THEN THEY WAITED...
AT NIGHTFALL, POLYPHEMOS RETURNED WITH HIS FLOCK,
ATE TWO MORE MEN...
AND ODYSSEUS SET HIS PLAN INTO MOTION.
HERE, O CYCLOPS, HAVE A DRINK.

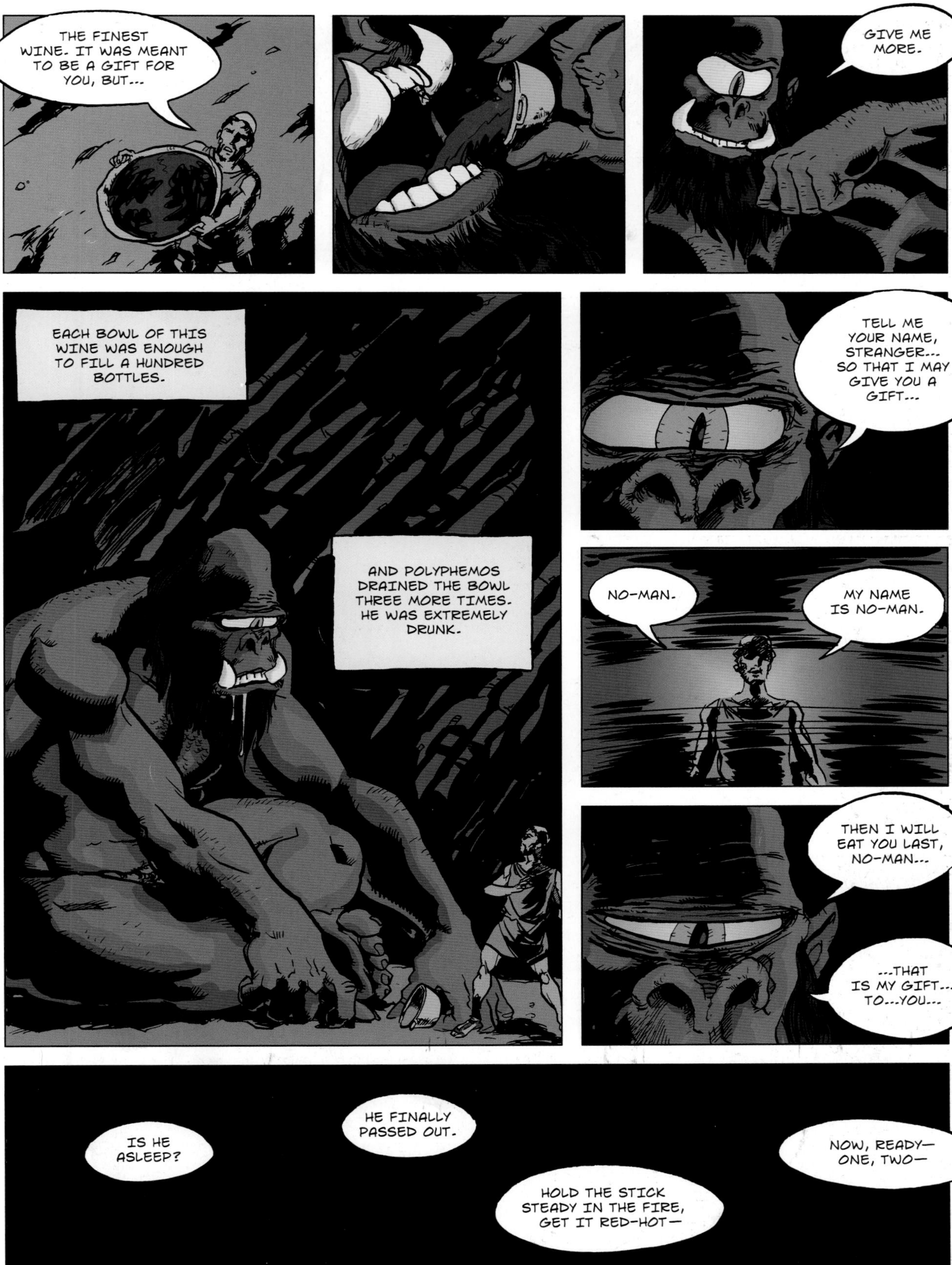
THE FINEST WINE. IT WAS MEANT TO BE A GIFT FOR YOU, BUT...
GIVE ME MORE.
EACH BOWL OF THIS WINE WAS ENOUGH TO FILL A HUNDRED BOTTLES.
AND POLYPHEMOS DRAINED THE BOWL THREE MORE TIMES. HE WAS EXTREMELY DRUNK.
TELL ME YOUR NAME, STRANGER... SO THAT I MAY GIVE YOU A GIFT...
NO-MAN.
MY NAME IS NO-MAN.
THEN I WILL EAT YOU LAST, NO-MAN...
...THAT IS MY GIFT... TO...YOU...
IS HE ASLEEP?
HE FINALLY PASSED OUT.
HOLD THE STICK STEADY IN THE FIRE, GET IT RED-HOT—
NOW, READY— ONE, TWO—

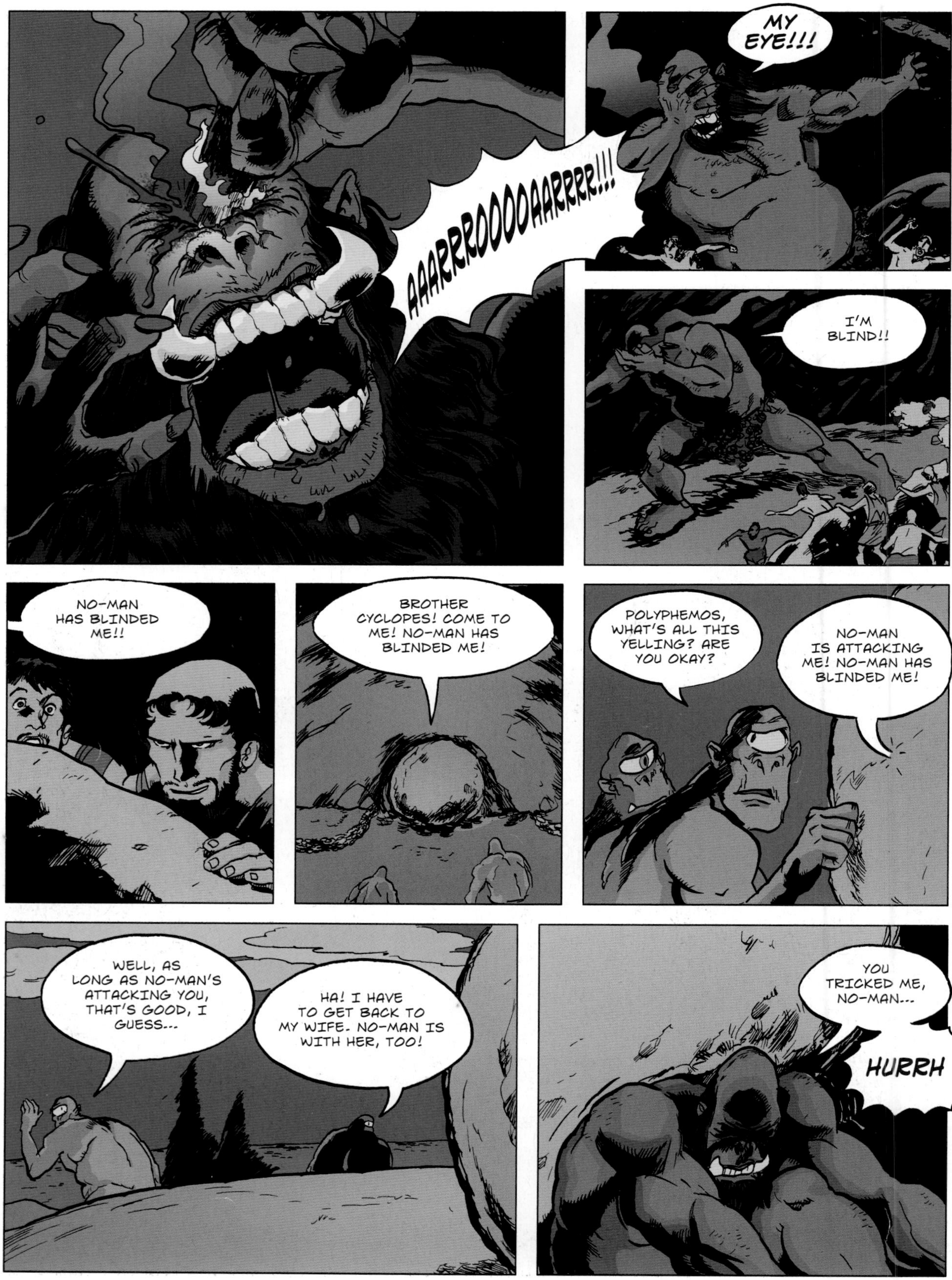
AAARRROOOOAARRRR!!!
MY EYE!!!
I'M BLIND!!
NO-MAN HAS BLINDED ME!!
BROTHER CYCLOPES! COME TO ME! NO-MAN HAS BLINDED ME!
POLYPHEMOS, WHAT'S ALL THIS YELLING? ARE YOU OKAY?
NO-MAN IS ATTACKING ME! NO-MAN HAS BLINDED ME!
WELL, AS LONG AS NO-MAN'S ATTACKING YOU, THAT'S GOOD, I GUESS...
HA! I HAVE TO GET BACK TO MY WIFE. NO-MAN IS WITH HER, TOO!
YOU TRICKED ME, NO-MAN...
HURRH

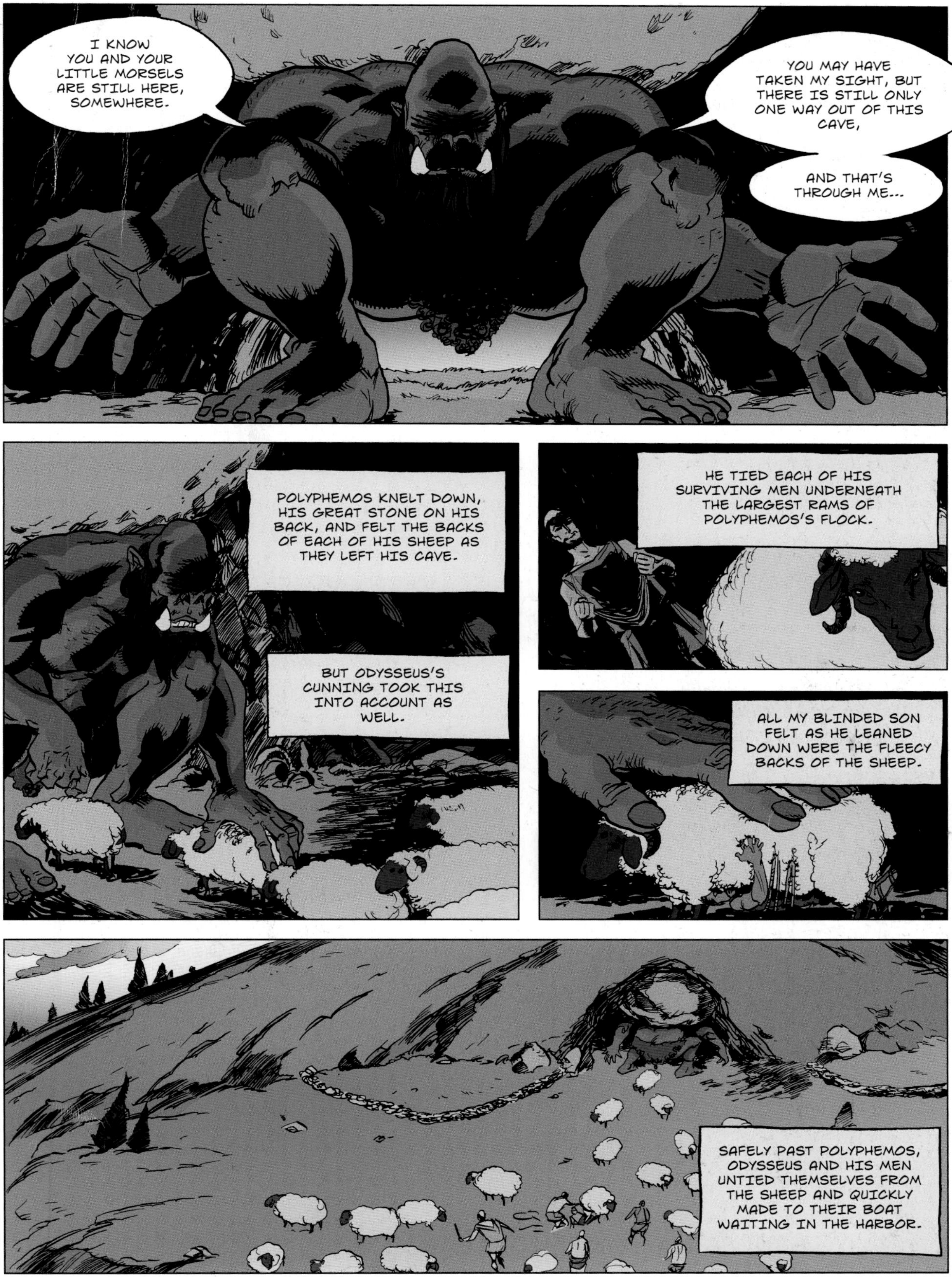
I KNOW YOU AND YOUR LITTLE MORSELS ARE STILL HERE, SOMEWHERE.
YOU MAY HAVE TAKEN MY SIGHT, BUT THERE IS STILL ONLY ONE WAY OUT OF THIS CAVE,
AND THAT'S THROUGH ME...
POLYPHEMOS KNELT DOWN, HIS GREAT STONE ON HIS BACK, AND FELT THE BACKS OF EACH OF HIS SHEEP AS THEY LEFT HIS CAVE.
BUT ODYSSEUS'S CUNNING TOOK THIS INTO ACCOUNT AS WELL.
HE TIED EACH OF HIS SURVIVING MEN UNDERNEATH THE LARGEST RAMS OF POLYPHEMOS'S FLOCK.
ALL MY BLINDED SON FELT AS HE LEANED DOWN WERE THE FLEECY BACKS OF THE SHEEP.
SAFELY PAST POLYPHEMOS, ODYSSEUS AND HIS MEN UNTIED THEMSELVES FROM THE SHEEP AND QUICKLY MADE TO THEIR BOAT WAITING IN THE HARBOR.

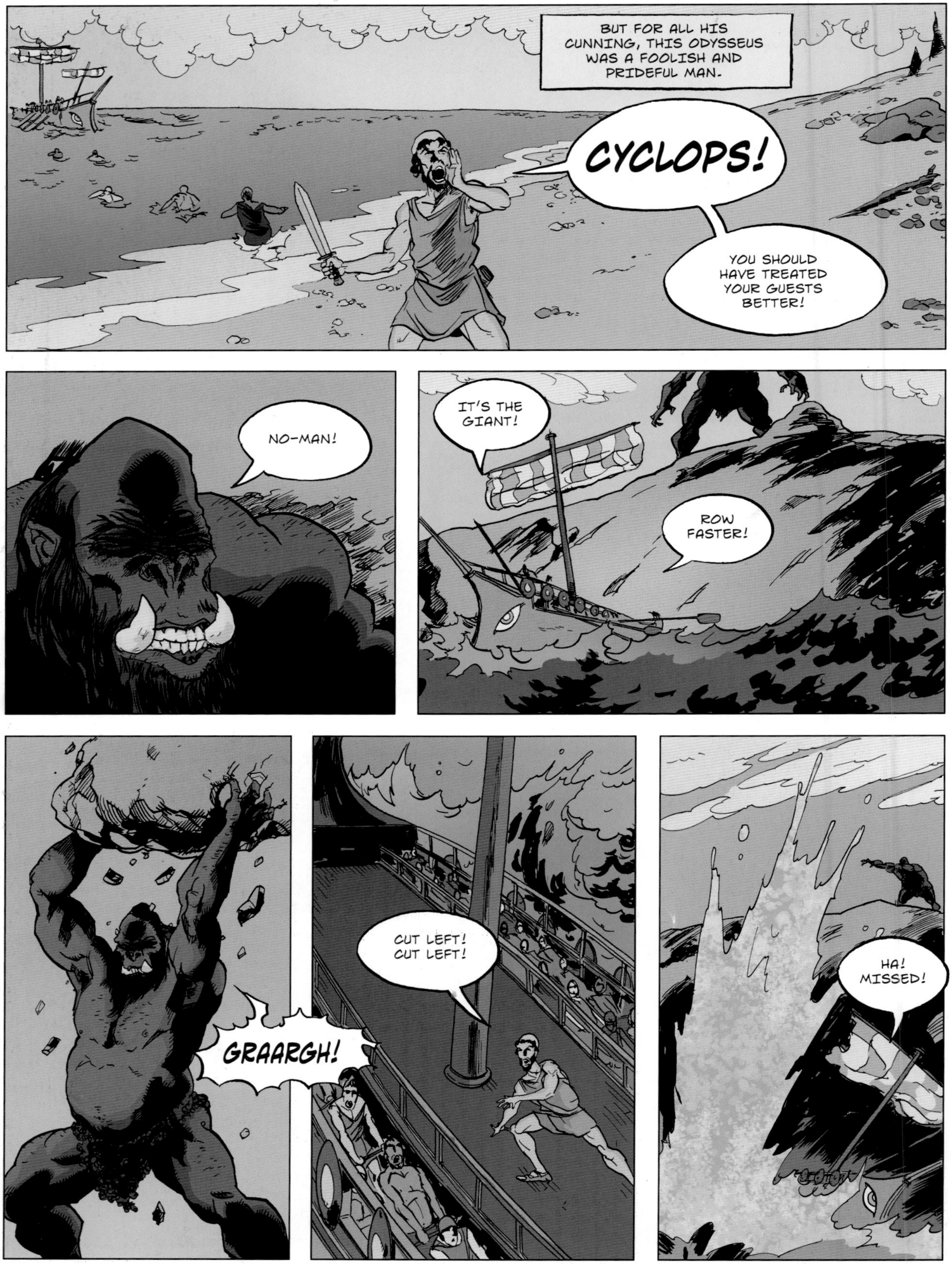
BUT FOR ALL HIS CUNNING, THIS ODYSSEUS WAS A FOOLISH AND PRIDEFUL MAN.
CYCLOPS!
YOU SHOULD HAVE TREATED YOUR GUESTS BETTER!
NO-MAN!
IT'S THE GIANT!
ROW FASTER!
GRAARGH!
CUT LEFT! CUT LEFT!
HA! MISSED!

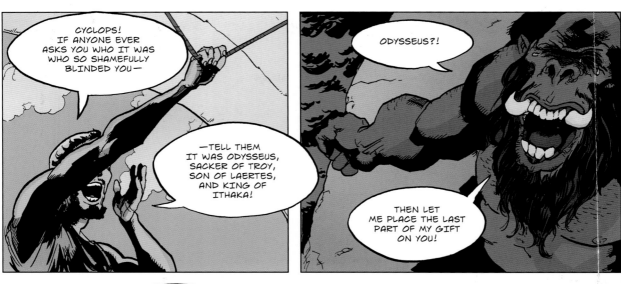

CYCLOPS! IF ANYONE EVER ASKS YOU WHO IT WAS WHO SO SHAMEFULLY BLINDED YOU—

—TELL THEM IT WAS ODYSSEUS, SACKER OF TROY, SON OF LAERTES, AND KING OF ITHAKA!

ODYSSEUS?!

THEN LET ME PLACE THE LAST PART OF MY GIFT ON YOU!

FOR MY FATHER IS POSEIDON THE EARTH SHAKER HIMSELF!

HEAR ME, O FATHER! I KNOW NOT IF YOU CAN HEAL MY EYE—

BUT I ASK YOU, MAKE IT THAT THIS ODYSSEUS SHALL NEVER RETURN TO HIS HOME IN ITHAKA!

AND IF HE MUST, LET IT BE LATE, AFTER THE LOSS OF HIS COMPANIONS, AND MAY HE FIND TROUBLES IN HIS HOME!

AND DEEP, DEEP BENEATH THE WINE-DARK SEA—

I HEARD MY SON'S PRAYER.

FOR TEN YEARS I DELAYED THE RETURN OF ODYSSEUS TO HIS HOME AND FAMILY ON ITHAKA.

AND WHEN HE FINALLY DID ARRIVE, THERE WAS MUCH TROUBLE IN HIS HOUSEHOLD, AND IT WAS AFTER THE LOSS OF ALL OF HIS COMPANIONS.

FOR THOUGH HE WAS MONSTROUS, POLYPHEMOS WAS MY SON...

AND MY CHILDREN HAVE ALWAYS TENDED TO BE MONSTROUS.

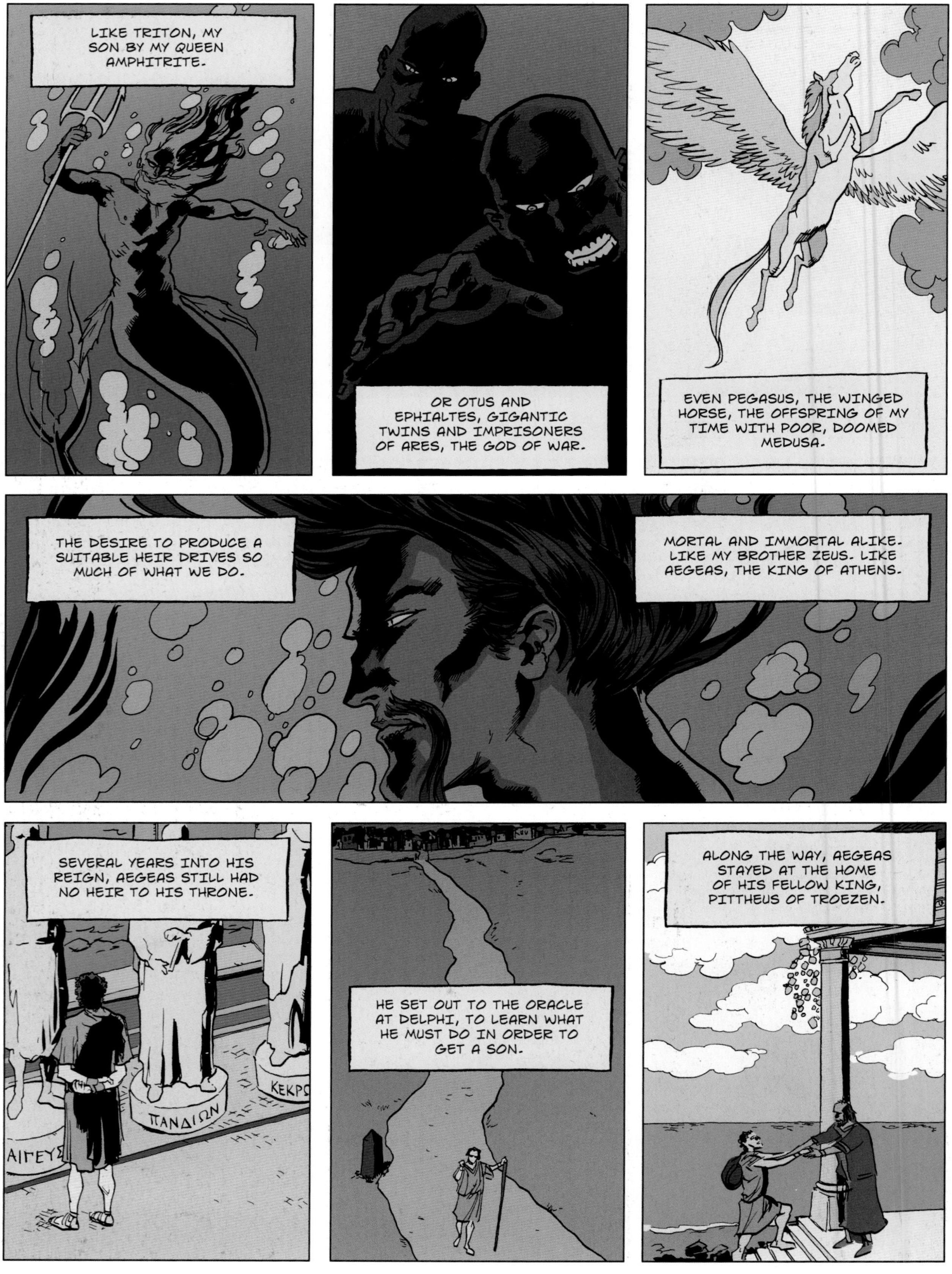
LIKE TRITON, MY SON BY MY QUEEN AMPHITRITE.
OR OTUS AND EPHIALTES, GIGANTIC TWINS AND IMPRISONERS OF ARES, THE GOD OF WAR.
EVEN PEGASUS, THE WINGED HORSE, THE OFFSPRING OF MY TIME WITH POOR, DOOMED MEDUSA.
THE DESIRE TO PRODUCE A SUITABLE HEIR DRIVES SO MUCH OF WHAT WE DO.
MORTAL AND IMMORTAL ALIKE. LIKE MY BROTHER ZEUS. LIKE AEGEAS, THE KING OF ATHENS.
SEVERAL YEARS INTO HIS REIGN, AEGEAS STILL HAD NO HEIR TO HIS THRONE.
ΚΕΚΡΟ
ΠΑΝΔΙΩΝ
ΑΙΓΕΥΣ
HE SET OUT TO THE ORACLE AT DELPHI, TO LEARN WHAT HE MUST DO IN ORDER TO GET A SON.
ALONG THE WAY, AEGEAS STAYED AT THE HOME OF HIS FELLOW KING, PITTHEUS OF TROEZEN.

IT WAS THERE HE MET AETHRA, DAUGHTER OF PITTHEUS.

HER BEAUTY SHONE LIKE THE MOON ON THE SEA.

AEGEAS WAS WITH HER THEN, IN TROEZEN.

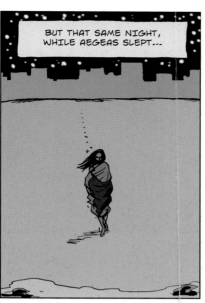

BUT THAT SAME NIGHT, WHILE AEGEAS SLEPT...

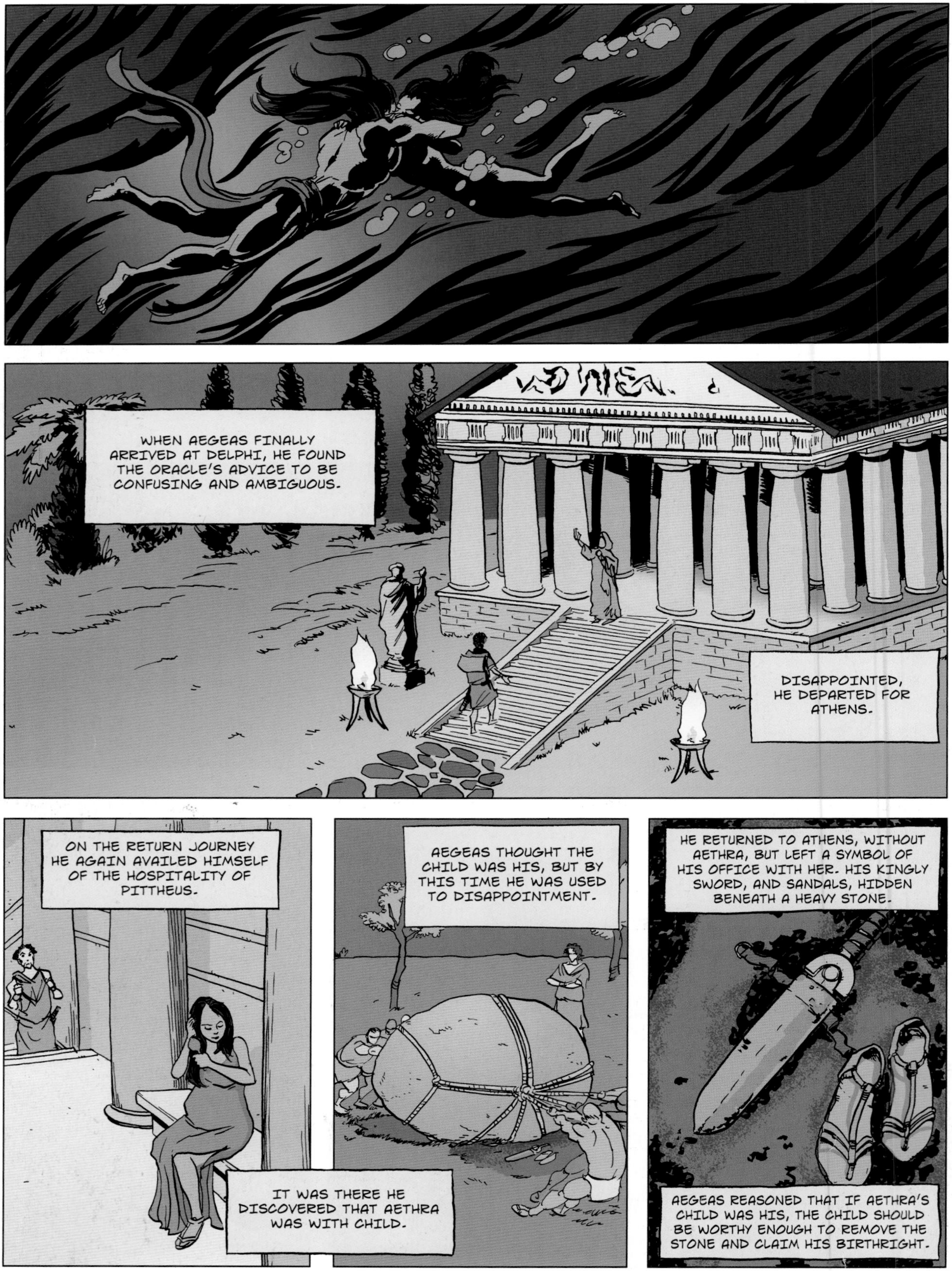
WHEN AEGEAS FINALLY ARRIVED AT DELPHI, HE FOUND THE ORACLE'S ADVICE TO BE CONFUSING AND AMBIGUOUS.
DISAPPOINTED, HE DEPARTED FOR ATHENS.
ON THE RETURN JOURNEY HE AGAIN AVAILED HIMSELF OF THE HOSPITALITY OF PITTHEUS.
IT WAS THERE HE DISCOVERED THAT AETHRA WAS WITH CHILD.
AEGEAS THOUGHT THE CHILD WAS HIS, BUT BY THIS TIME HE WAS USED TO DISAPPOINTMENT.
HE RETURNED TO ATHENS, WITHOUT AETHRA, BUT LEFT A SYMBOL OF HIS OFFICE WITH HER. HIS KINGLY SWORD, AND SANDALS, HIDDEN BENEATH A HEAVY STONE.
AEGEAS REASONED THAT IF AETHRA'S CHILD WAS HIS, THE CHILD SHOULD BE WORTHY ENOUGH TO REMOVE THE STONE AND CLAIM HIS BIRTHRIGHT.

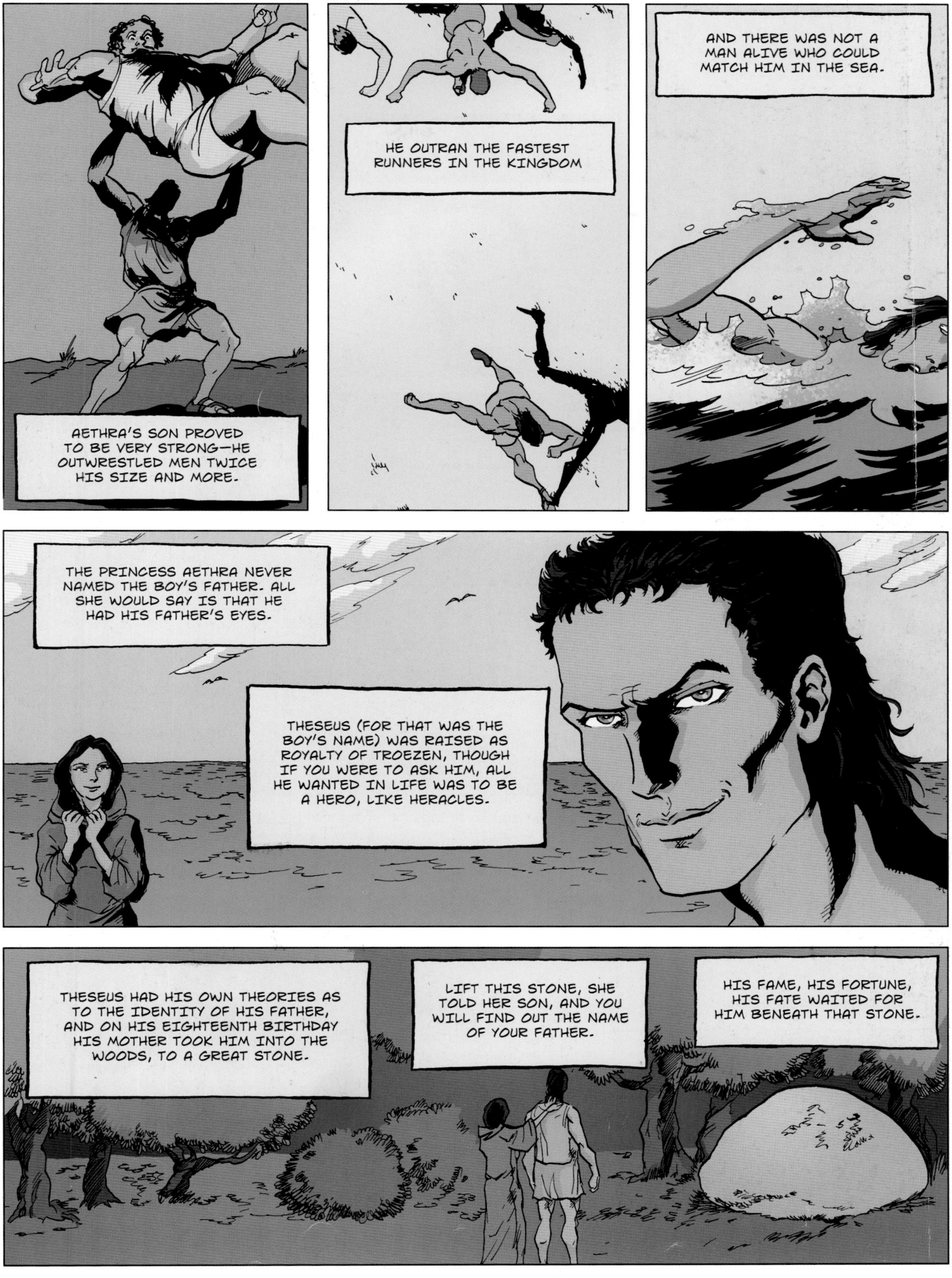
AETHRA'S SON PROVED TO BE VERY STRONG—HE OUTWRESTLED MEN TWICE HIS SIZE AND MORE.
HE OUTRAN THE FASTEST RUNNERS IN THE KINGDOM
AND THERE WAS NOT A MAN ALIVE WHO COULD MATCH HIM IN THE SEA.
THE PRINCESS AETHRA NEVER NAMED THE BOY'S FATHER. ALL SHE WOULD SAY IS THAT HE HAD HIS FATHER'S EYES.
THESEUS (FOR THAT WAS THE BOY'S NAME) WAS RAISED AS ROYALTY OF TROEZEN, THOUGH IF YOU WERE TO ASK HIM, ALL HE WANTED IN LIFE WAS TO BE A HERO, LIKE HERACLES.
THESEUS HAD HIS OWN THEORIES AS TO THE IDENTITY OF HIS FATHER, AND ON HIS EIGHTEENTH BIRTHDAY HIS MOTHER TOOK HIM INTO THE WOODS, TO A GREAT STONE.
LIFT THIS STONE, SHE TOLD HER SON, AND YOU WILL FIND OUT THE NAME OF YOUR FATHER.
HIS FAME, HIS FORTUNE, HIS FATE WAITED FOR HIM BENEATH THAT STONE.

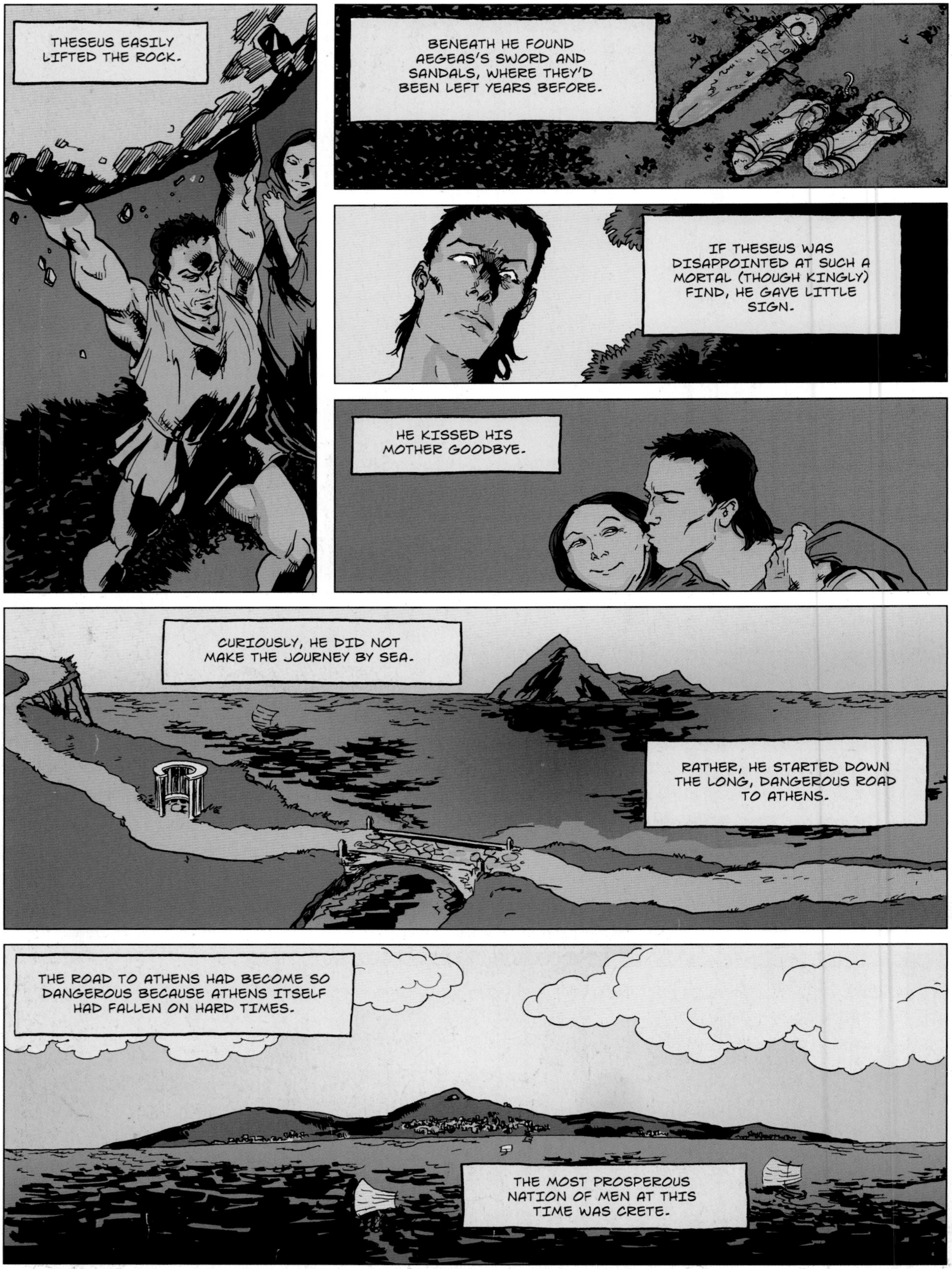
THESEUS EASILY LIFTED THE ROCK.
BENEATH HE FOUND AEGEAS'S SWORD AND SANDALS, WHERE THEY'D BEEN LEFT YEARS BEFORE.
IF THESEUS WAS DISAPPOINTED AT SUCH A MORTAL (THOUGH KINGLY) FIND, HE GAVE LITTLE SIGN.
HE KISSED HIS MOTHER GOODBYE.
CURIOUSLY, HE DID NOT MAKE THE JOURNEY BY SEA.
RATHER, HE STARTED DOWN THE LONG, DANGEROUS ROAD TO ATHENS.
THE ROAD TO ATHENS HAD BECOME SO DANGEROUS BECAUSE ATHENS ITSELF HAD FALLEN ON HARD TIMES.
THE MOST PROSPEROUS NATION OF MEN AT THIS TIME WAS CRETE.

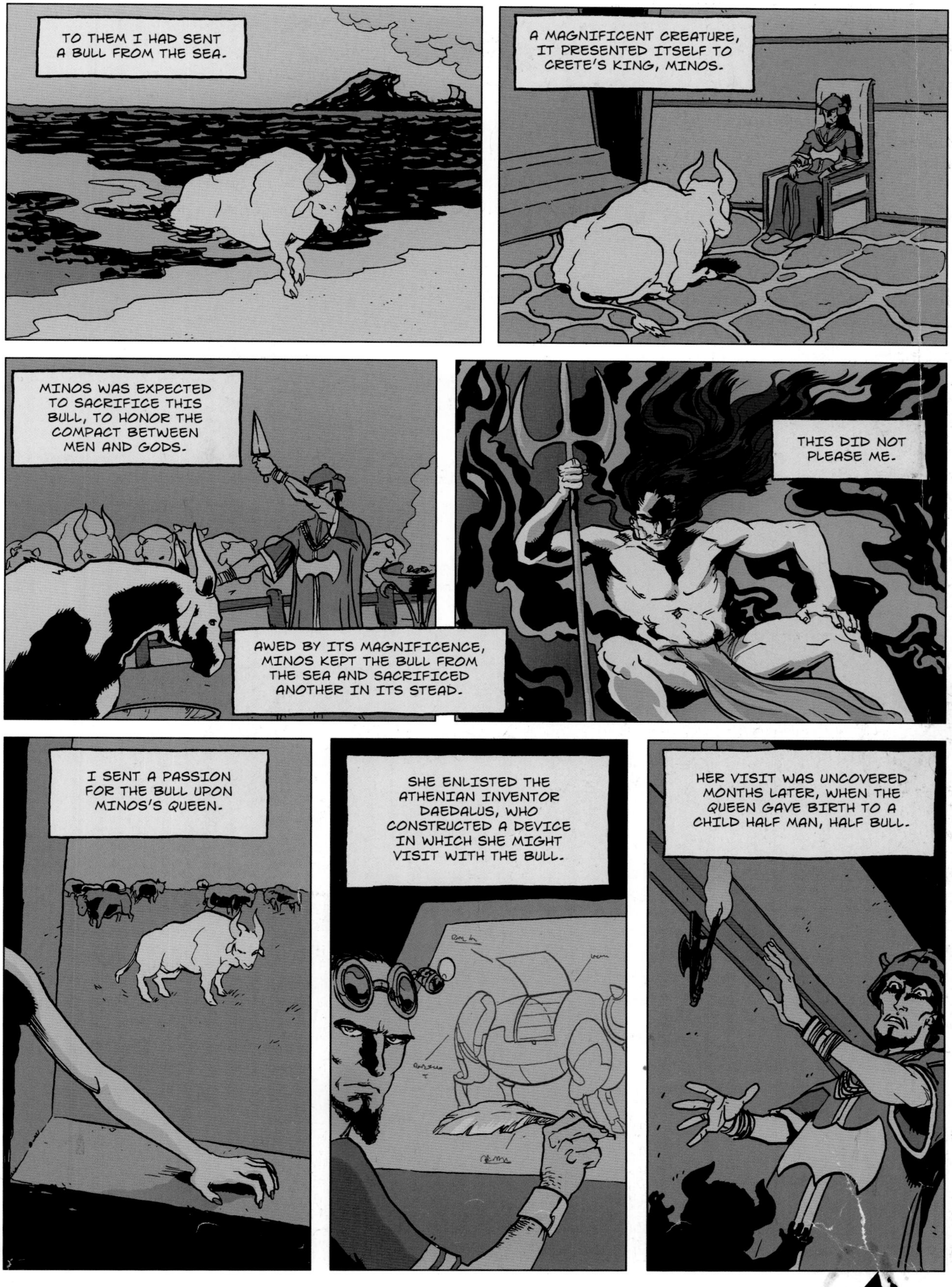

TO THEM I HAD SENT A BULL FROM THE SEA.
A MAGNIFICENT CREATURE, IT PRESENTED ITSELF TO CRETE'S KING, MINOS.
MINOS WAS EXPECTED TO SACRIFICE THIS BULL, TO HONOR THE COMPACT BETWEEN MEN AND GODS.
AWED BY ITS MAGNIFICENCE, MINOS KEPT THE BULL FROM THE SEA AND SACRIFICED ANOTHER IN ITS STEAD.
THIS DID NOT PLEASE ME.
I SENT A PASSION FOR THE BULL UPON MINOS'S QUEEN.
SHE ENLISTED THE ATHENIAN INVENTOR DAEDALUS, WHO CONSTRUCTED A DEVICE IN WHICH SHE MIGHT VISIT WITH THE BULL.
HER VISIT WAS UNCOVERED MONTHS LATER, WHEN THE QUEEN GAVE BIRTH TO A CHILD HALF MAN, HALF BULL.

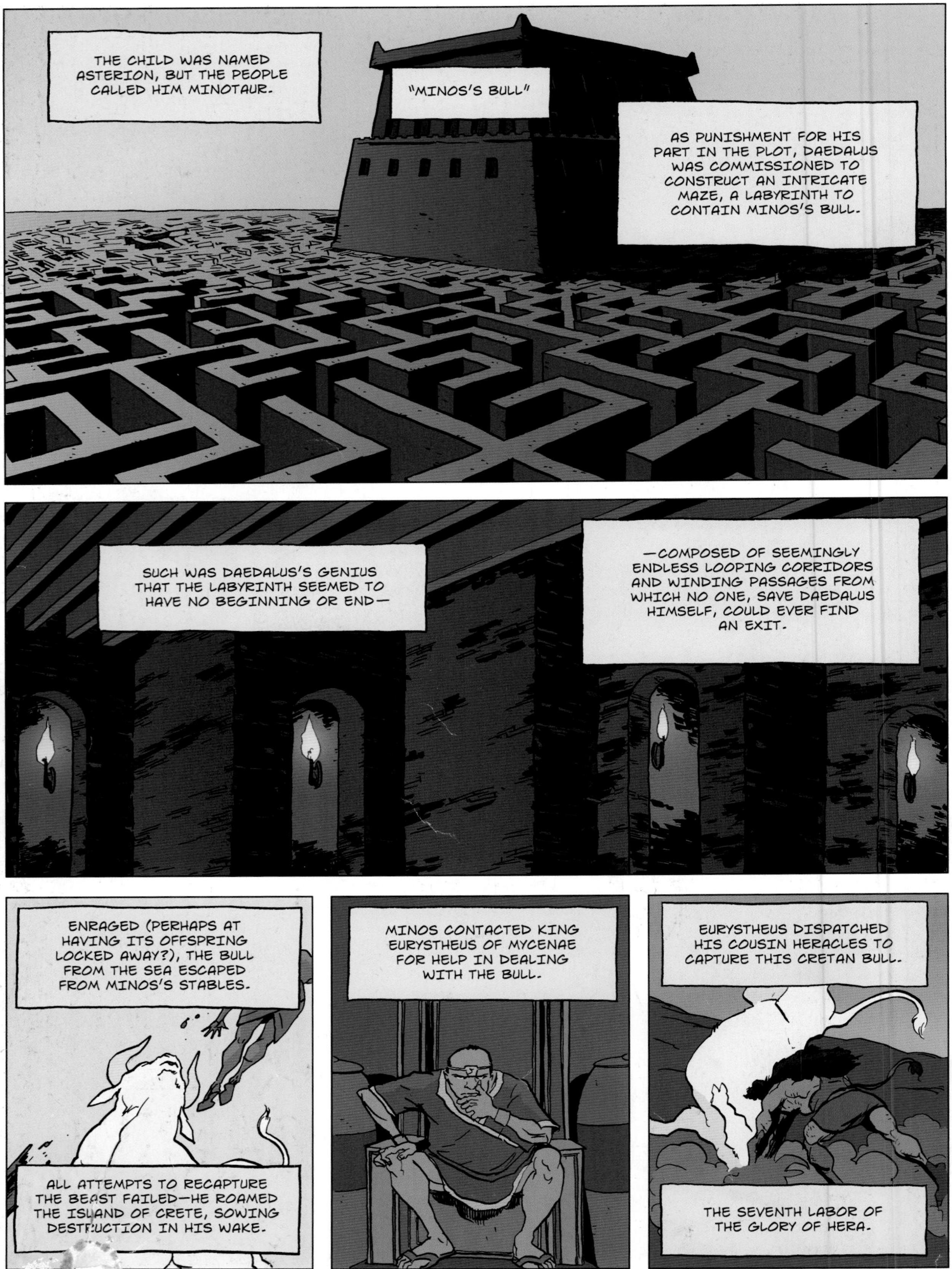
THE CHILD WAS NAMED ASTERION, BUT THE PEOPLE CALLED HIM MINOTAUR.
"MINOS'S BULL"
AS PUNISHMENT FOR HIS PART IN THE PLOT, DAEDALUS WAS COMMISSIONED TO CONSTRUCT AN INTRICATE MAZE, A LABYRINTH TO CONTAIN MINOS'S BULL.
SUCH WAS DAEDALUS'S GENIUS THAT THE LABYRINTH SEEMED TO HAVE NO BEGINNING OR END—
—COMPOSED OF SEEMINGLY ENDLESS LOOPING CORRIDORS AND WINDING PASSAGES FROM WHICH NO ONE, SAVE DAEDALUS HIMSELF, COULD EVER FIND AN EXIT.
ENRAGED (PERHAPS AT HAVING ITS OFFSPRING LOCKED AWAY?), THE BULL FROM THE SEA ESCAPED FROM MINOS'S STABLES.
ALL ATTEMPTS TO RECAPTURE THE BEAST FAILED—HE ROAMED THE ISLAND OF CRETE, SOWING DESTRUCTION IN HIS WAKE.
MINOS CONTACTED KING EURYSTHEUS OF MYCENAE FOR HELP IN DEALING WITH THE BULL.
EURYSTHEUS DISPATCHED HIS COUSIN HERACLES TO CAPTURE THIS CRETAN BULL.
THE SEVENTH LABOR OF THE GLORY OF HERA.

HERACLES HAD THE BULL SHIPPED TO ATHENS AND OUT OF MINOS'S HAIR.

BUT I WASN'T DONE WITH MINOS YET...

ONCE IN ATHENS, THE BULL ESCAPED AGAIN.

IN NEARBY MARATHON, AEGEAS WAS HOLDING GAMES TO HONOR THE GODS.

THE BULL TRAMPLED THE VISITING SON OF MINOS TO DEATH.

GRIEF-STRICKEN, MINOS BROUGHT THE FULL MIGHT OF THE CRETAN NAVY AGAINST ATHENS, AND SUBJUGATED THE CITY.

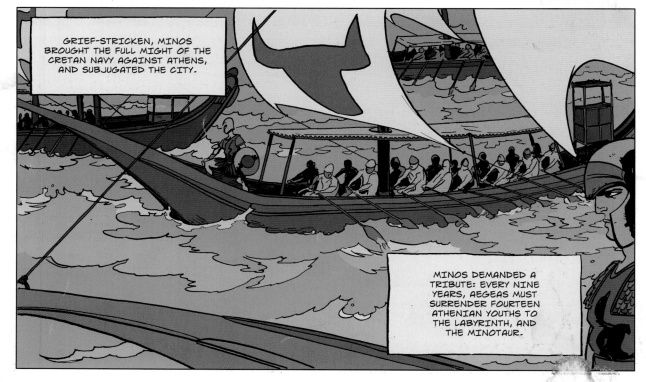

MINOS DEMANDED A TRIBUTE: EVERY NINE YEARS, AEGEAS MUST SURRENDER FOURTEEN ATHENIAN YOUTHS TO THE LABYRINTH, AND THE MINOTAUR.

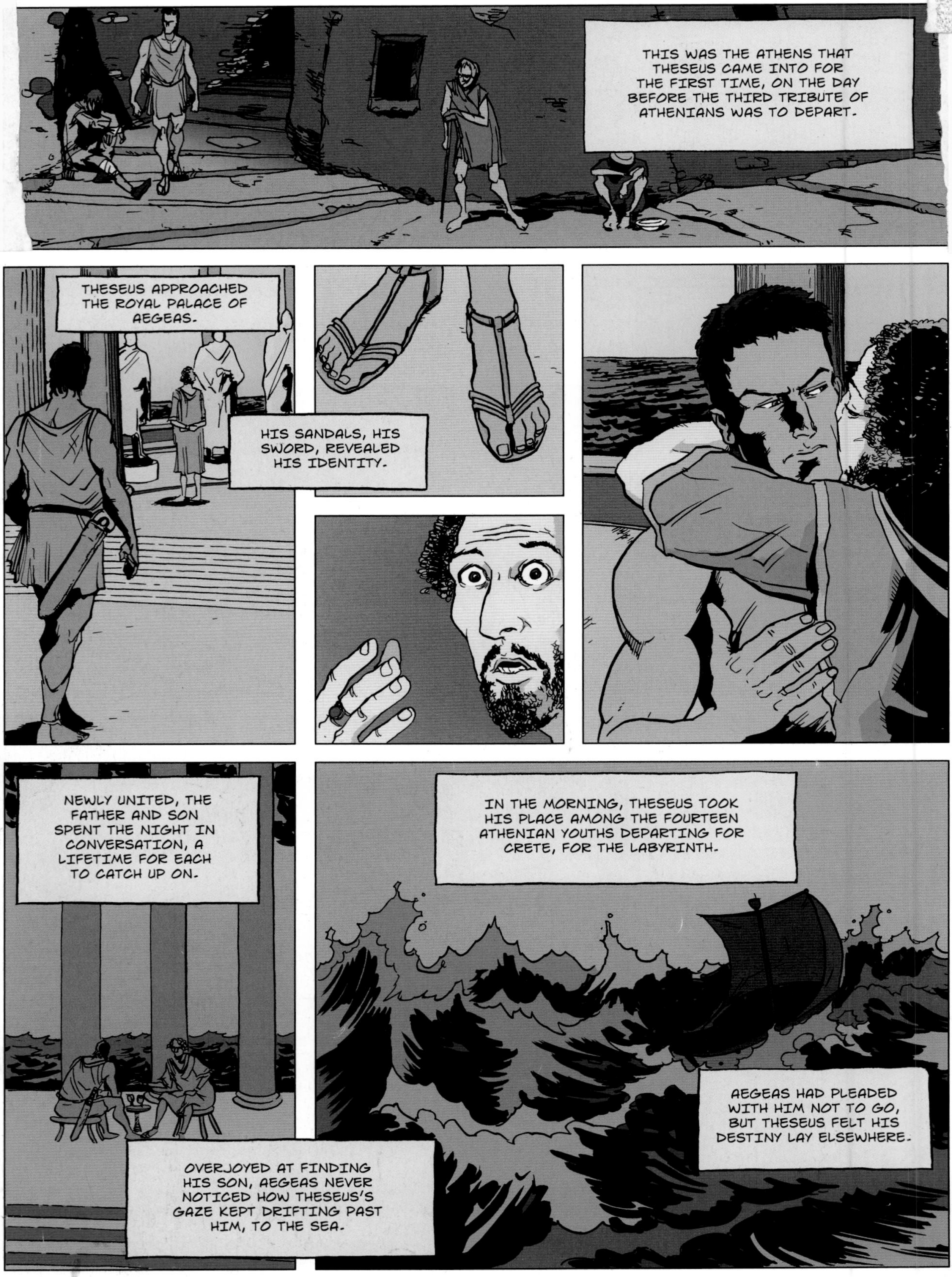

THIS WAS THE ATHENS THAT THESEUS CAME INTO FOR THE FIRST TIME, ON THE DAY BEFORE THE THIRD TRIBUTE OF ATHENIANS WAS TO DEPART.
THESEUS APPROACHED THE ROYAL PALACE OF AEGEAS.
HIS SANDALS, HIS SWORD, REVEALED HIS IDENTITY.
NEWLY UNITED, THE FATHER AND SON SPENT THE NIGHT IN CONVERSATION, A LIFETIME FOR EACH TO CATCH UP ON.
OVERJOYED AT FINDING HIS SON, AEGEAS NEVER NOTICED HOW THESEUS'S GAZE KEPT DRIFTING PAST HIM, TO THE SEA.
IN THE MORNING, THESEUS TOOK HIS PLACE AMONG THE FOURTEEN ATHENIAN YOUTHS DEPARTING FOR CRETE, FOR THE LABYRINTH.
AEGEAS HAD PLEADED WITH HIM NOT TO GO, BUT THESEUS FELT HIS DESTINY LAY ELSEWHERE.

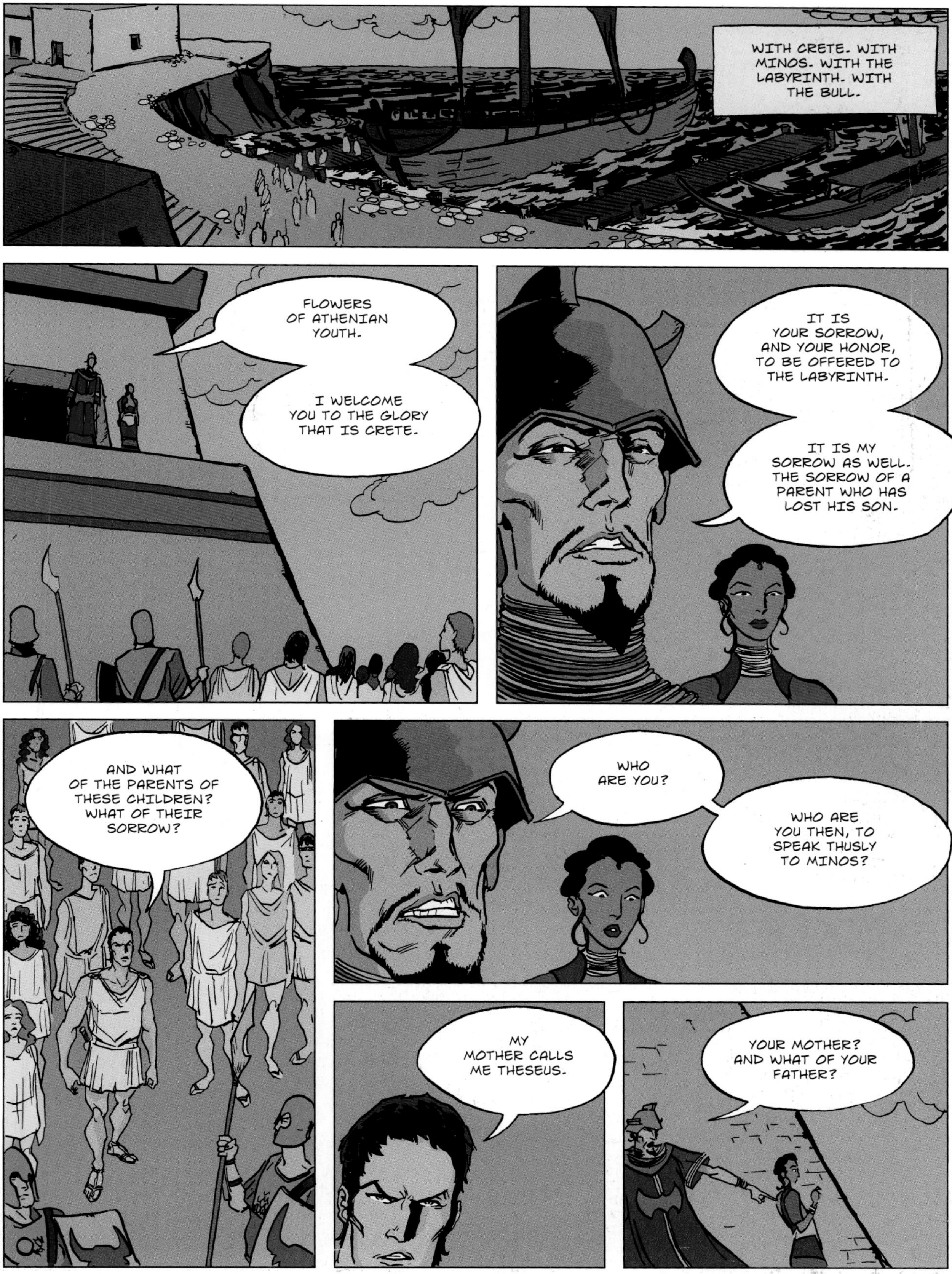
WITH CRETE. WITH MINOS. WITH THE LABYRINTH. WITH THE BULL.
FLOWERS OF ATHENIAN YOUTH.
I WELCOME YOU TO THE GLORY THAT IS CRETE.
IT IS YOUR SORROW, AND YOUR HONOR, TO BE OFFERED TO THE LABYRINTH.
IT IS MY SORROW AS WELL. THE SORROW OF A PARENT WHO HAS LOST HIS SON.
AND WHAT OF THE PARENTS OF THESE CHILDREN? WHAT OF THEIR SORROW?
WHO ARE YOU?
WHO ARE YOU THEN, TO SPEAK THUSLY TO MINOS?
MY MOTHER CALLS ME THESEUS.
YOUR MOTHER? AND WHAT OF YOUR FATHER?

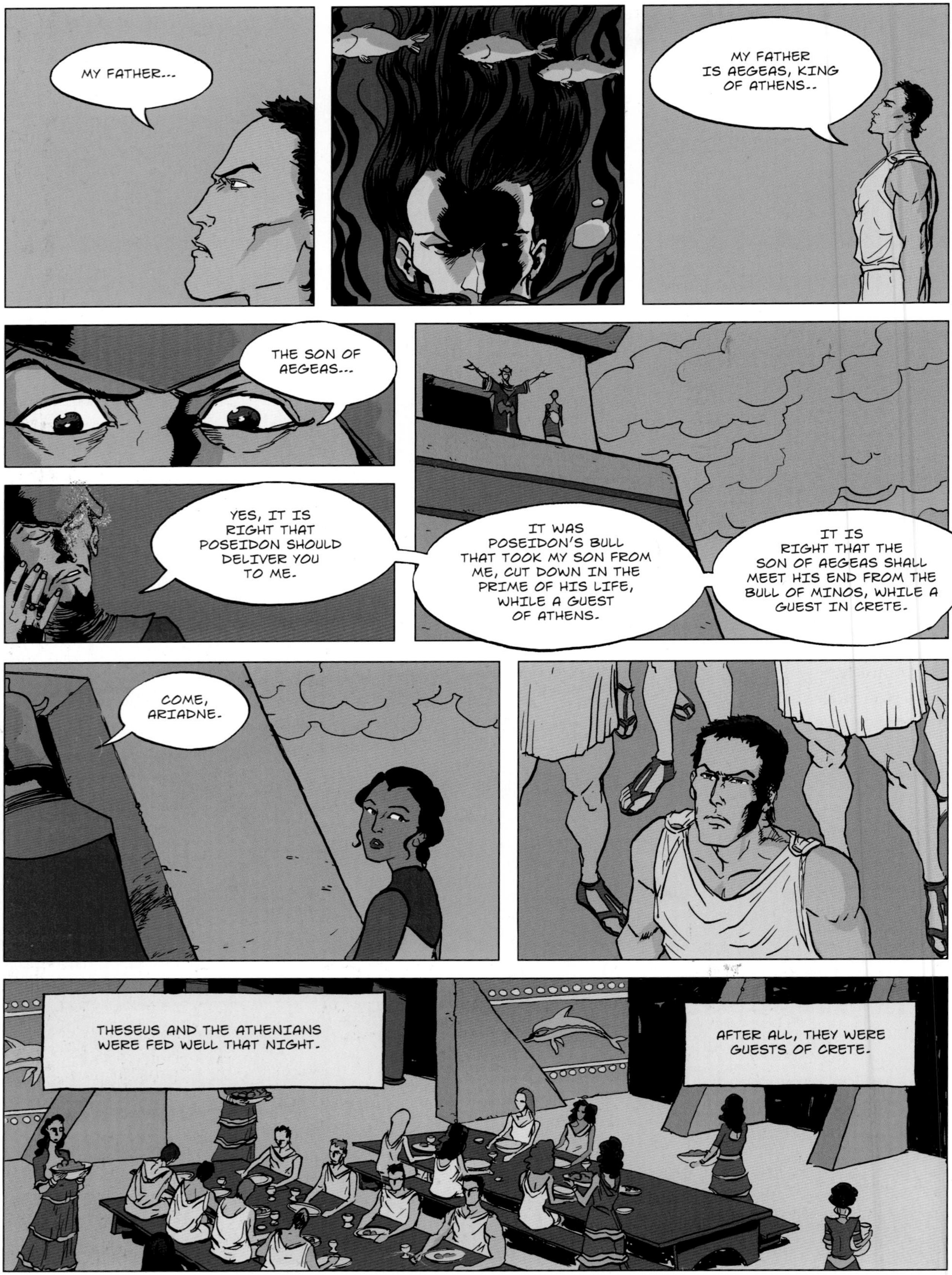
MY FATHER...
MY FATHER IS AEGEAS, KING OF ATHENS..
THE SON OF AEGEAS...
YES, IT IS RIGHT THAT POSEIDON SHOULD DELIVER YOU TO ME.
IT WAS POSEIDON'S BULL THAT TOOK MY SON FROM ME, CUT DOWN IN THE PRIME OF HIS LIFE, WHILE A GUEST OF ATHENS.
IT IS RIGHT THAT THE SON OF AEGEAS SHALL MEET HIS END FROM THE BULL OF MINOS, WHILE A GUEST IN CRETE.
COME, ARIADNE.
THESEUS AND THE ATHENIANS WERE FED WELL THAT NIGHT.
AFTER ALL, THEY WERE GUESTS OF CRETE.

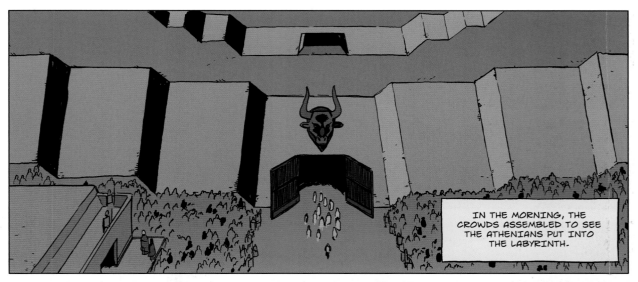

IN THE MORNING, THE CROWDS ASSEMBLED TO SEE THE ATHENIANS PUT INTO THE LABYRINTH.

HOLD, THESEUS.

TO KEEP YOU WARM, IN THE LABYRINTH.

YOUR SWORD IS HIDDEN IN THIS CLOAK. I SOMEHOW DOUBT THAT ASTERION WILL BE THE END OF YOU.

BUT THE LABYRINTH WILL NOT BE SO EASILY CONQUERED.

I ALSO GAVE YOU A SPOOL OF THREAD. TIE ONE END TO THE INSIDE DOOR OF THE LABYRINTH. IT WILL GUIDE YOU BACK TO SAFETY.

I SENSE YOU ARE MORE, SOMEHOW, THAN JUST AEGEAS'S SON, THESEUS.

GOOD LUCK.

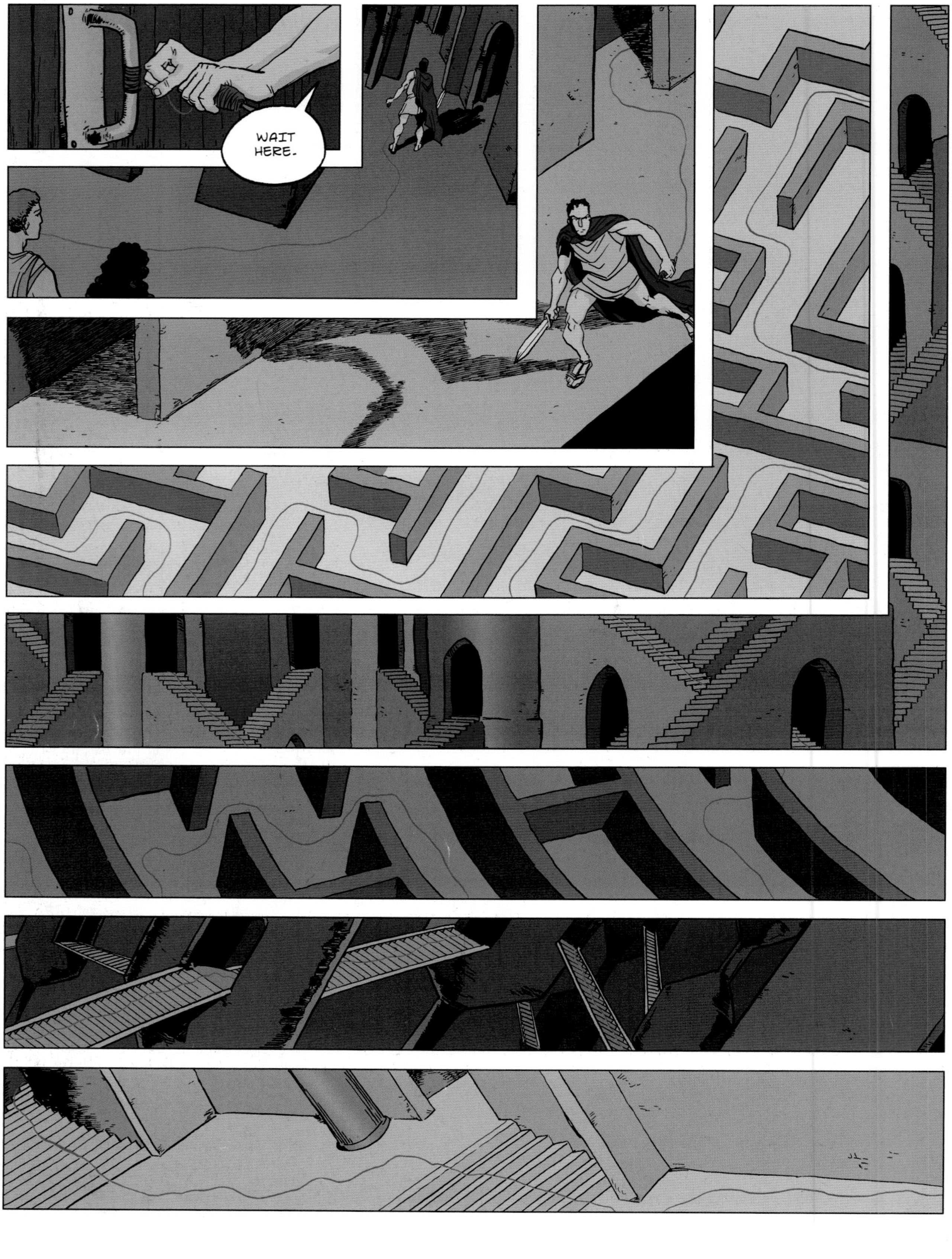
WAIT HERE.

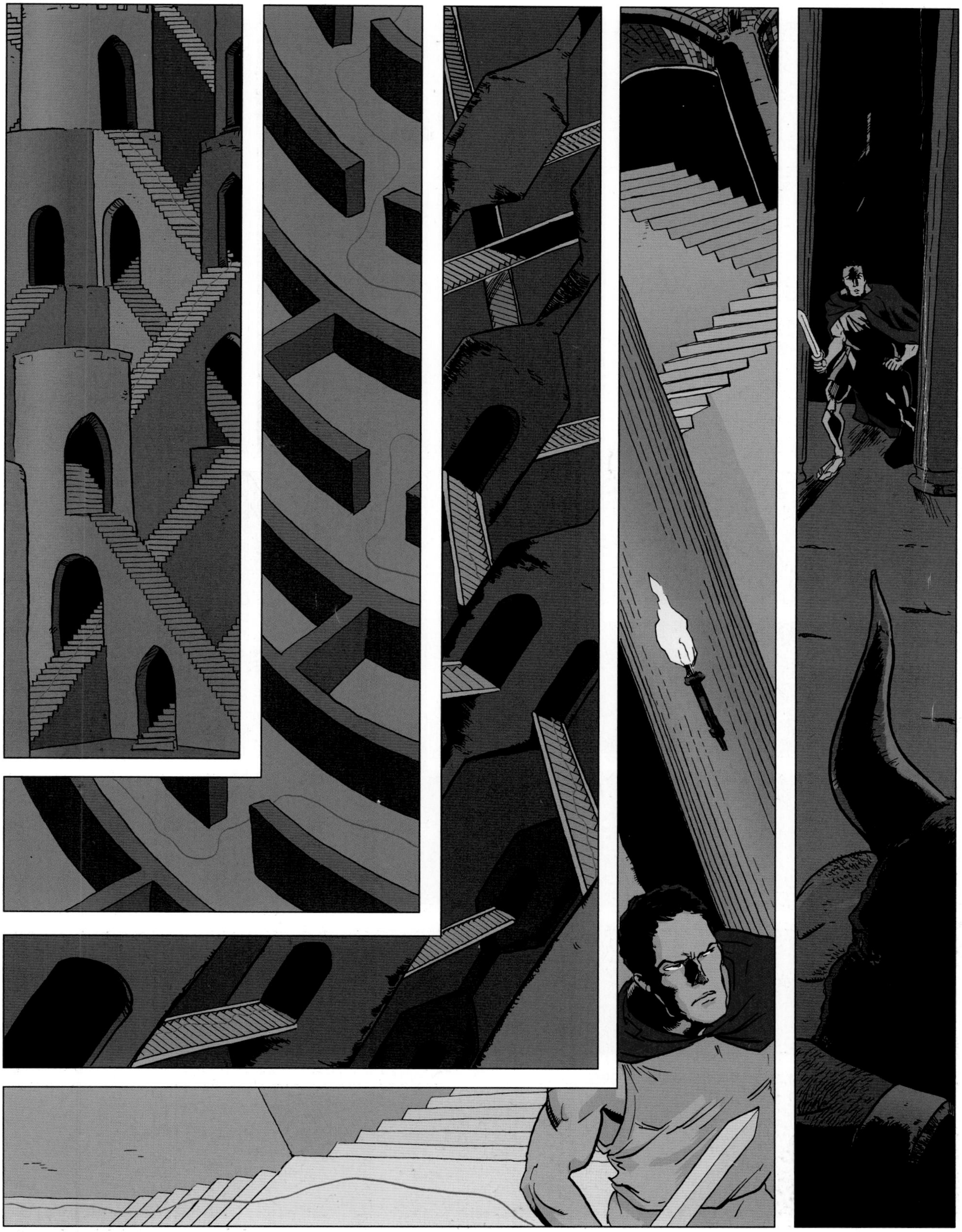

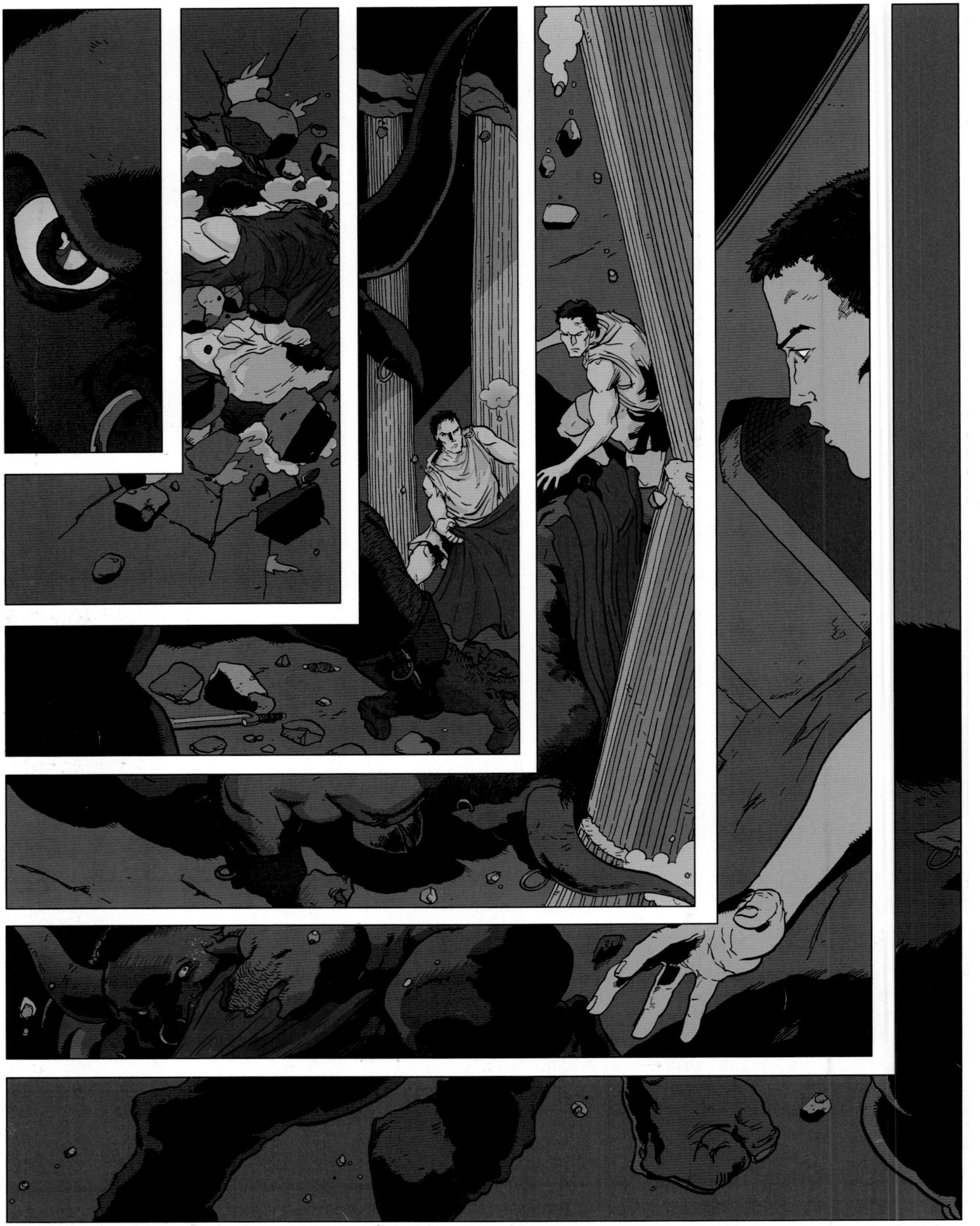

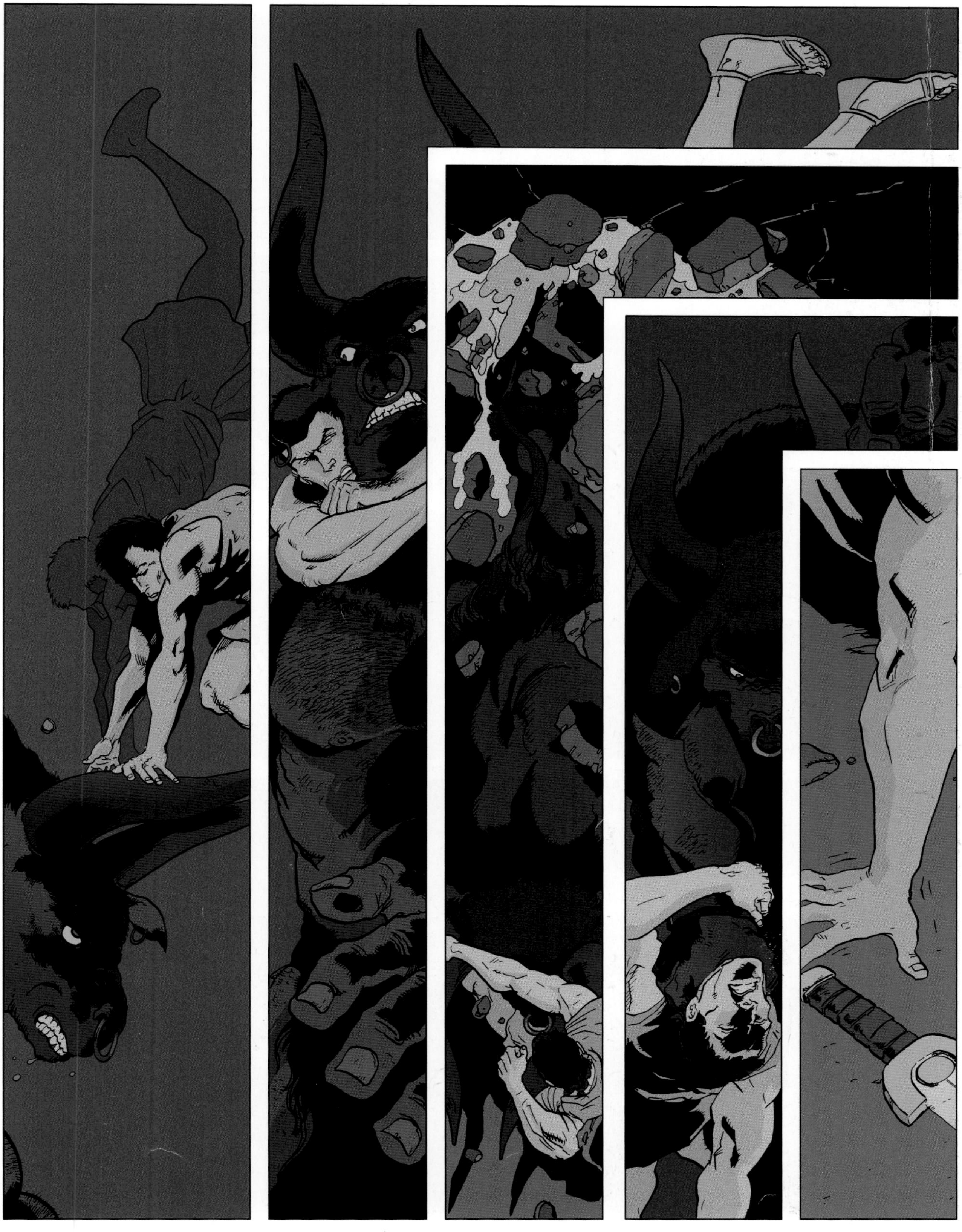

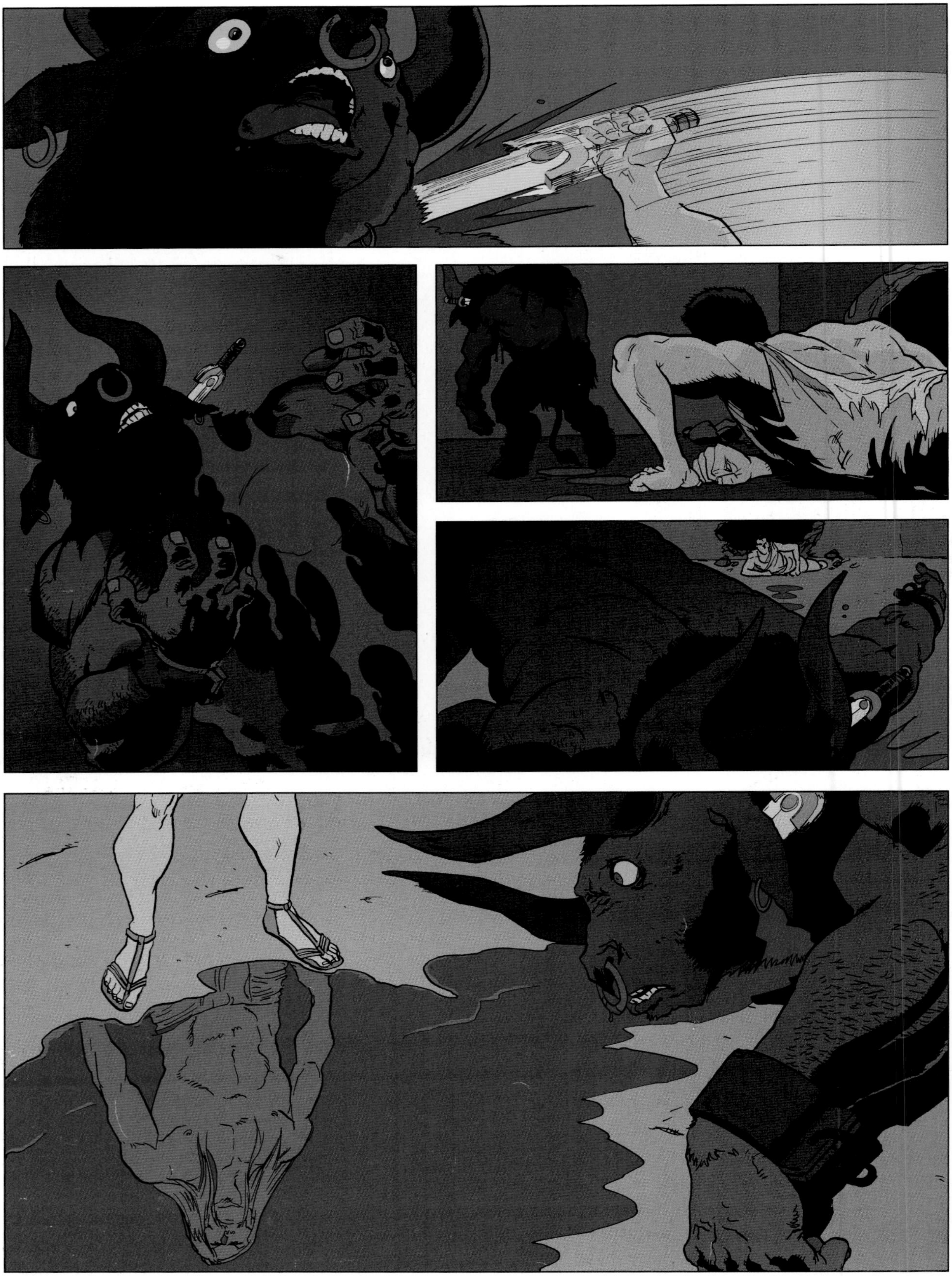

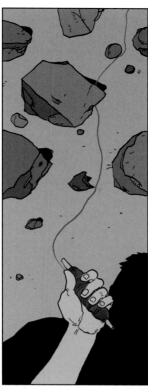

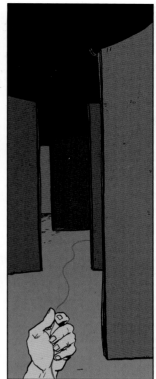

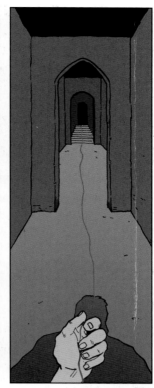

CAN YOU BELIEVE IT, ARIADNE?

THE MINOTAUR BARELY DEFENDED HIMSELF.

HIS NAME WAS ASTERION.

WHEN WE WERE CHILDREN, FOR A TIME MY FATHER TRIED TO RAISE HIM WITH US, BEFORE HE GREW TOO BIG, TOO DANGEROUS...

I USED TO PUT FLOWERS ON HIS HORNS...

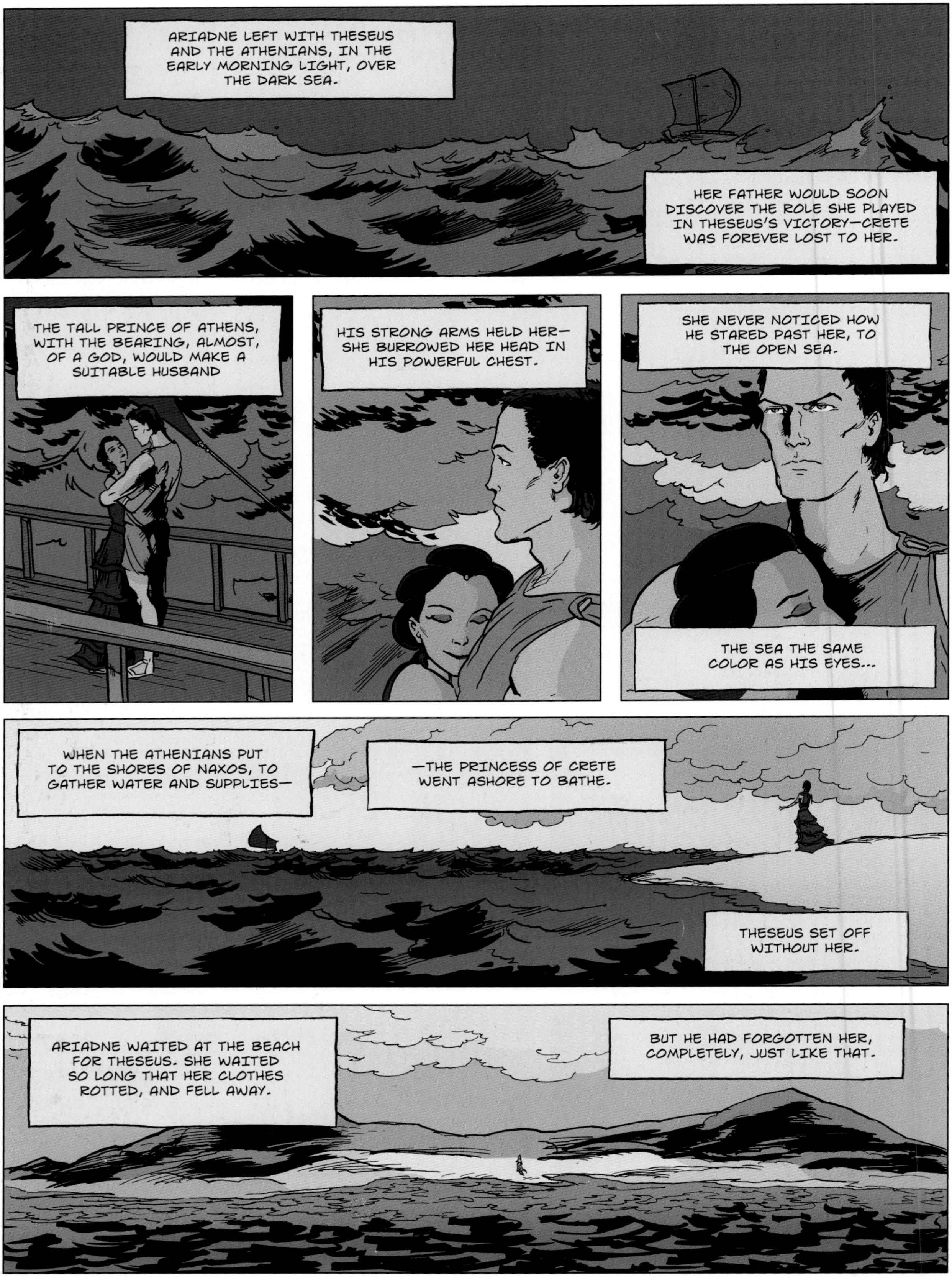
ARIADNE LEFT WITH THESEUS AND THE ATHENIANS, IN THE EARLY MORNING LIGHT, OVER THE DARK SEA.
HER FATHER WOULD SOON DISCOVER THE ROLE SHE PLAYED IN THESEUS'S VICTORY—CRETE WAS FOREVER LOST TO HER.
THE TALL PRINCE OF ATHENS, WITH THE BEARING, ALMOST, OF A GOD, WOULD MAKE A SUITABLE HUSBAND
HIS STRONG ARMS HELD HER—SHE BURROWED HER HEAD IN HIS POWERFUL CHEST.
SHE NEVER NOTICED HOW HE STARED PAST HER, TO THE OPEN SEA.
THE SEA THE SAME COLOR AS HIS EYES...
WHEN THE ATHENIANS PUT TO THE SHORES OF NAXOS, TO GATHER WATER AND SUPPLIES—
—THE PRINCESS OF CRETE WENT ASHORE TO BATHE.
THESEUS SET OFF WITHOUT HER.
ARIADNE WAITED AT THE BEACH FOR THESEUS. SHE WAITED SO LONG THAT HER CLOTHES ROTTED, AND FELL AWAY.
BUT HE HAD FORGOTTEN HER, COMPLETELY, JUST LIKE THAT.

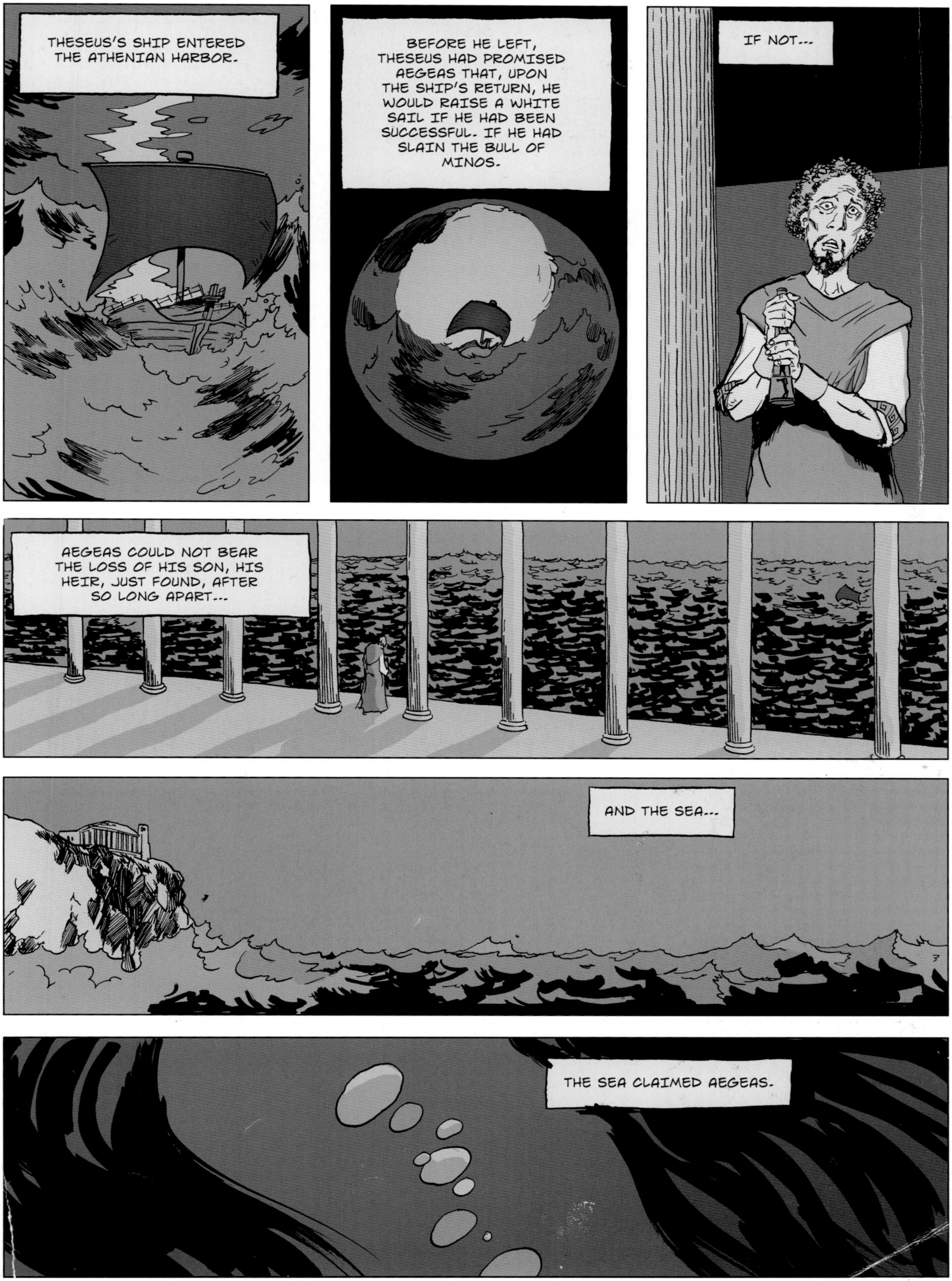
THESEUS'S SHIP ENTERED THE ATHENIAN HARBOR.
BEFORE HE LEFT, THESEUS HAD PROMISED AEGEAS THAT, UPON THE SHIP'S RETURN, HE WOULD RAISE A WHITE SAIL IF HE HAD BEEN SUCCESSFUL. IF HE HAD SLAIN THE BULL OF MINOS.
IF NOT...
AEGEAS COULD NOT BEAR THE LOSS OF HIS SON, HIS HEIR, JUST FOUND, AFTER SO LONG APART...
AND THE SEA...
THE SEA CLAIMED AEGEAS.

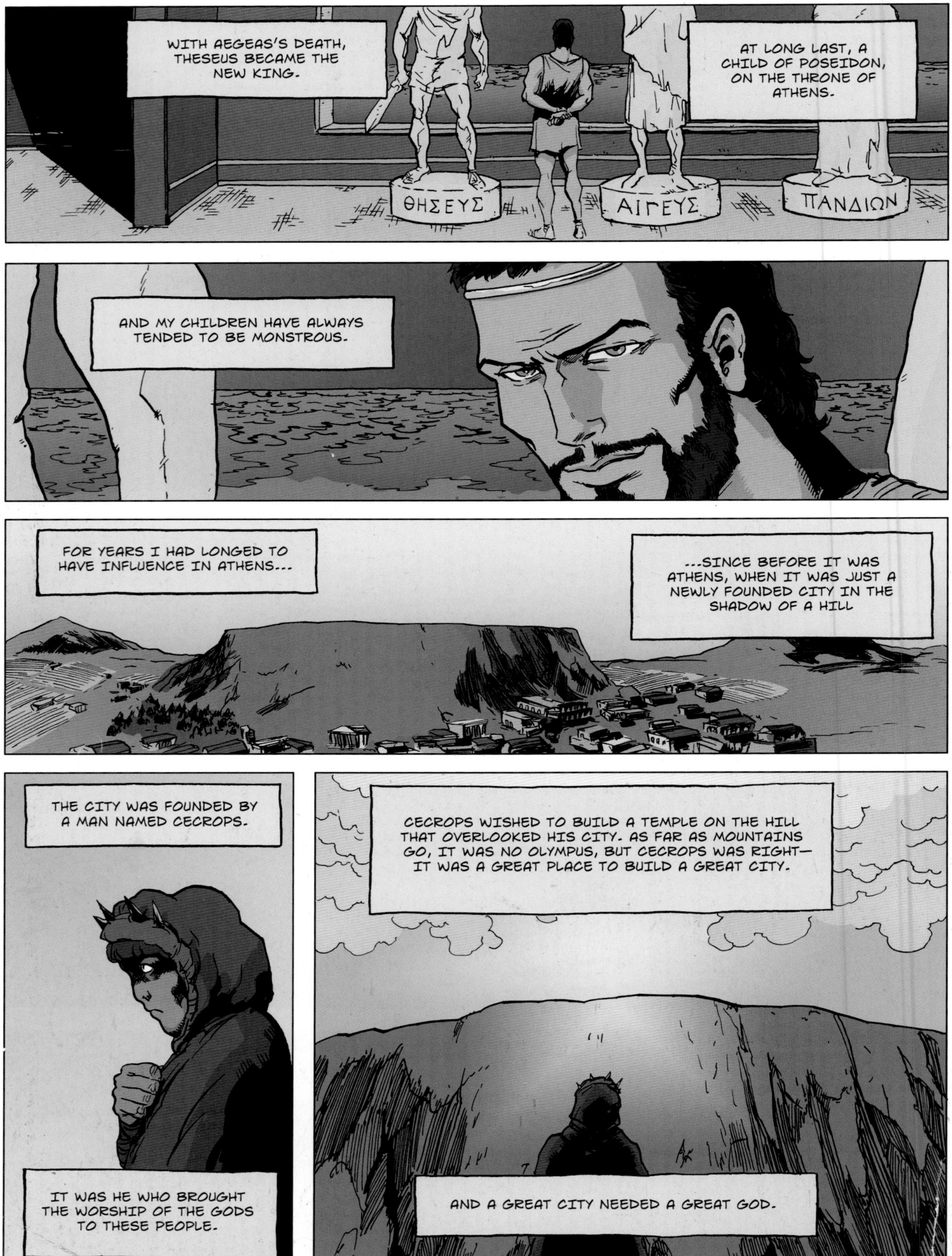
WITH AEGEAS'S DEATH, THESEUS BECAME THE NEW KING.
AT LONG LAST, A CHILD OF POSEIDON, ON THE THRONE OF ATHENS.
ΘΗΣΕΥΣ
ΑΙΓΕΥΣ
ΠΑΝΔΙΩΝ
AND MY CHILDREN HAVE ALWAYS TENDED TO BE MONSTROUS.
FOR YEARS I HAD LONGED TO HAVE INFLUENCE IN ATHENS...
...SINCE BEFORE IT WAS ATHENS, WHEN IT WAS JUST A NEWLY FOUNDED CITY IN THE SHADOW OF A HILL
THE CITY WAS FOUNDED BY A MAN NAMED CECROPS.
IT WAS HE WHO BROUGHT THE WORSHIP OF THE GODS TO THESE PEOPLE.
CECROPS WISHED TO BUILD A TEMPLE ON THE HILL THAT OVERLOOKED HIS CITY. AS FAR AS MOUNTAINS GO, IT WAS NO OLYMPUS, BUT CECROPS WAS RIGHT— IT WAS A GREAT PLACE TO BUILD A GREAT CITY.
AND A GREAT CITY NEEDED A GREAT GOD.

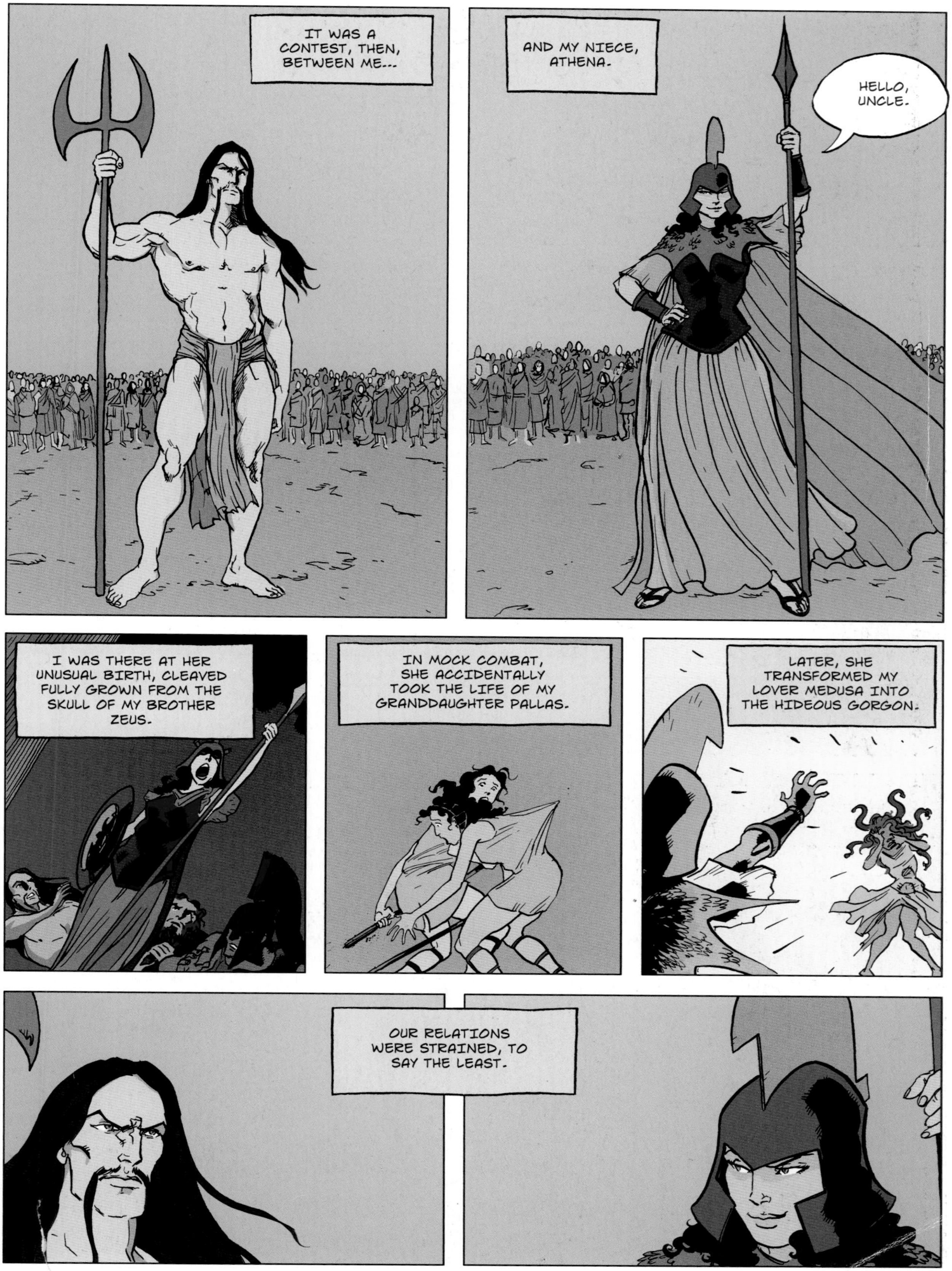
IT WAS A CONTEST, THEN, BETWEEN ME...
AND MY NIECE, ATHENA.
HELLO, UNCLE.
I WAS THERE AT HER UNUSUAL BIRTH, CLEAVED FULLY GROWN FROM THE SKULL OF MY BROTHER ZEUS.
IN MOCK COMBAT, SHE ACCIDENTALLY TOOK THE LIFE OF MY GRANDDAUGHTER PALLAS.
LATER, SHE TRANSFORMED MY LOVER MEDUSA INTO THE HIDEOUS GORGON.
OUR RELATIONS WERE STRAINED, TO SAY THE LEAST.

WE STOOD FACING EACH OTHER ATOP THE HILL THAT OVERLOOKED THE CITY.

WE WOULD EACH BESTOW A GIFT UPON THE CITIZENS OF THIS CITY. WHOSOEVER GAVE THE GREATER GIFT WOULD BECOME THE PATRON DEITY OF THE CITY.

AFTER YOU, UNCLE.

HMMPF!

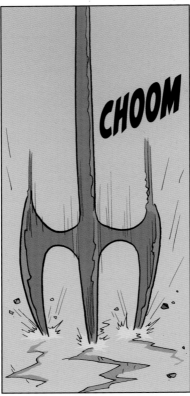

CHOOM

KK
KKKK
KRRRKK
KK.

FROOOSH

WATER!

MIGHTY POSEIDON HAS BLESSED US WITH THIS GLORIOUS GEYSER OF LIFE-GIVING WATER!

ALL HAIL LORD EARTH SHAKER!

GREAT POSEIDON, WHO GIVES US THIS CLEAR, BEAUTIFUL, DELICIOUS—

PFAAH!

SALT! THIS WATER IS SALTY!

MIGHTY POSEIDON, THE SPRING YOU HAVE CREATED FOR US, IT IS SEAWATER! IT—

UH...

WE HUMBLY THANK YOU FOR YOUR MOST GENEROUS GIFT, LORD EARTH SHAKER.

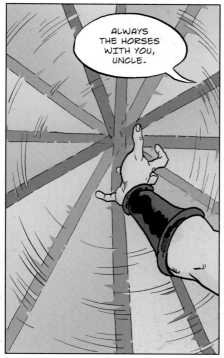

ALWAYS THE HORSES WITH YOU, UNCLE.

49

MY TURN NOW.

WHY A GOD OF THE SEA IS SO OBSESSED WITH HORSES, I'LL NEVER KNOW.

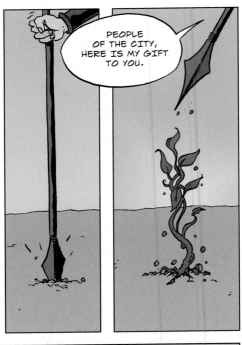

PEOPLE OF THE CITY, HERE IS MY GIFT TO YOU.

A TREE, CALLED THE OLIVE.

IT WILL GIVE YOU WOOD, AND THE FRUIT OF THIS TREE WILL YIELD AN OIL...

THIS OIL, IT CAN BE USED TO FEED YOU, TO CLEAN YOU, TO HEAL YOU...

THE FRUIT OF THIS TREE CAN ALSO BE EATEN.

POSEIDON'S GIFT IS NOT TOTALLY USELESS—THE BRINE OF HIS GEYSER CAN BE USED TO PICKLE THE FRUIT.

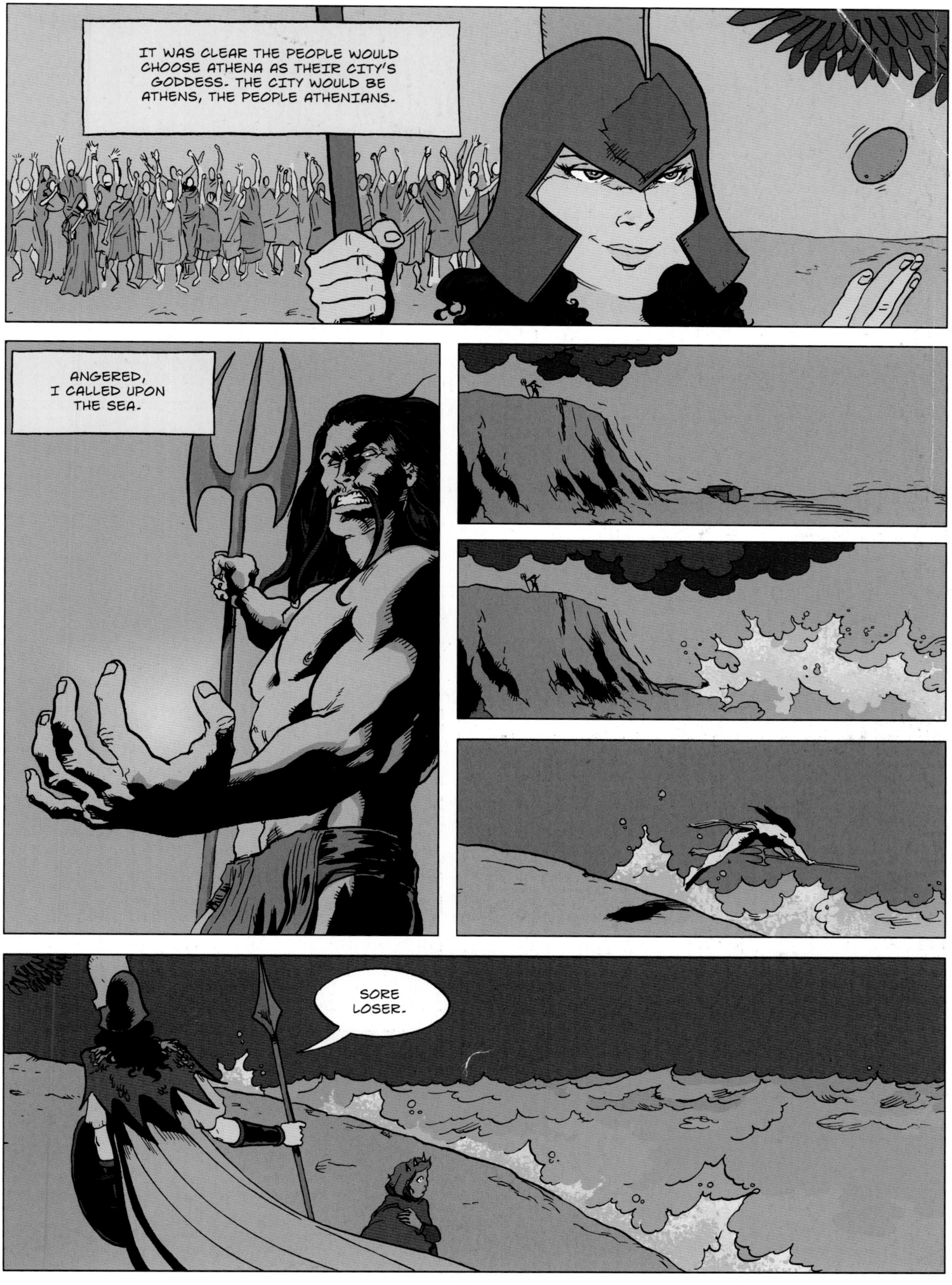
IT WAS CLEAR THE PEOPLE WOULD CHOOSE ATHENA AS THEIR CITY'S GODDESS. THE CITY WOULD BE ATHENS, THE PEOPLE ATHENIANS.
ANGERED, I CALLED UPON THE SEA.
SORE LOSER.

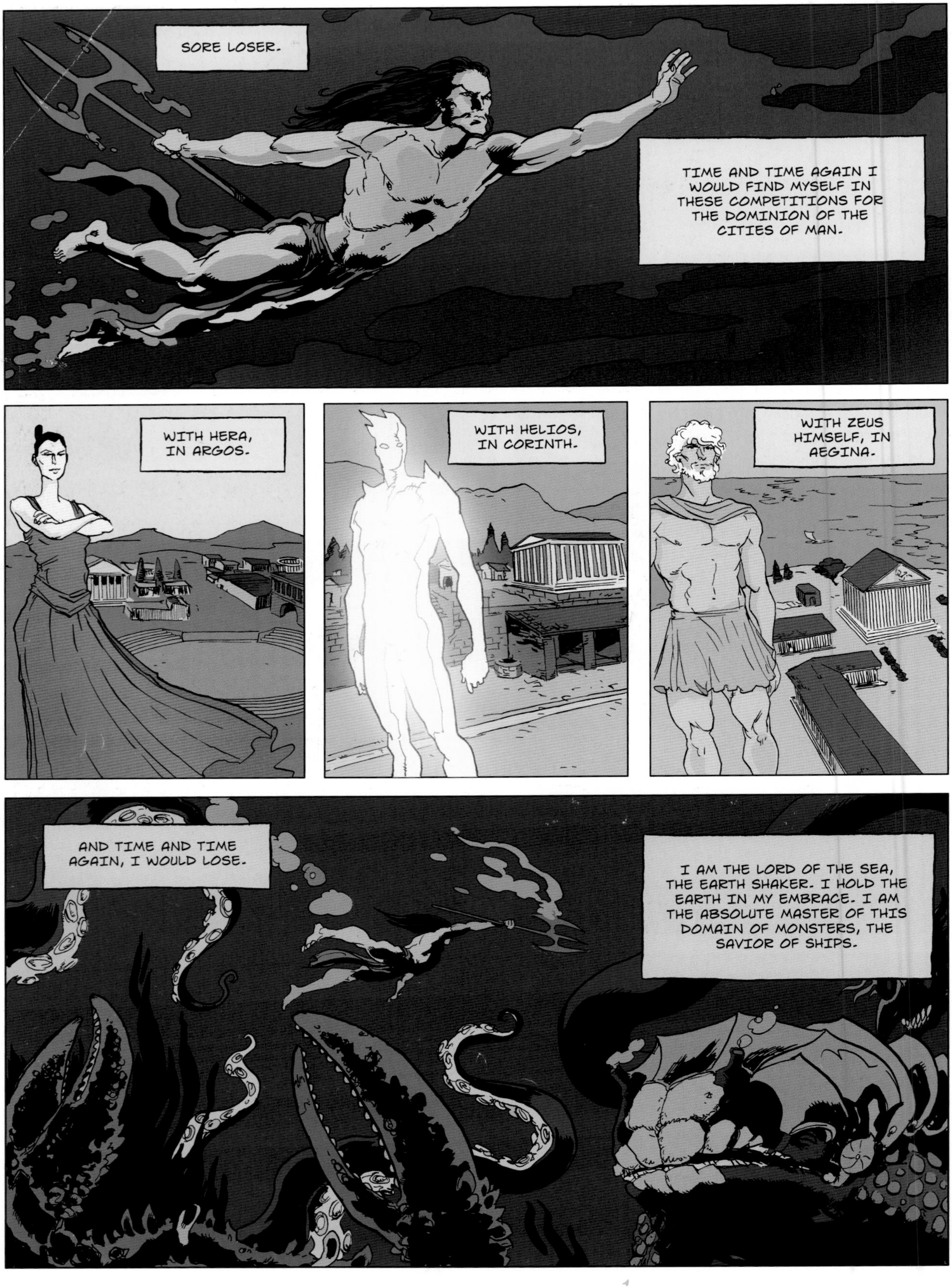
SORE LOSER.
TIME AND TIME AGAIN I WOULD FIND MYSELF IN THESE COMPETITIONS FOR THE DOMINION OF THE CITIES OF MAN.
WITH HERA, IN ARGOS.
WITH HELIOS, IN CORINTH.
WITH ZEUS HIMSELF, IN AEGINA.
AND TIME AND TIME AGAIN, I WOULD LOSE.
I AM THE LORD OF THE SEA, THE EARTH SHAKER. I HOLD THE EARTH IN MY EMBRACE. I AM THE ABSOLUTE MASTER OF THIS DOMAIN OF MONSTERS, THE SAVIOR OF SHIPS.

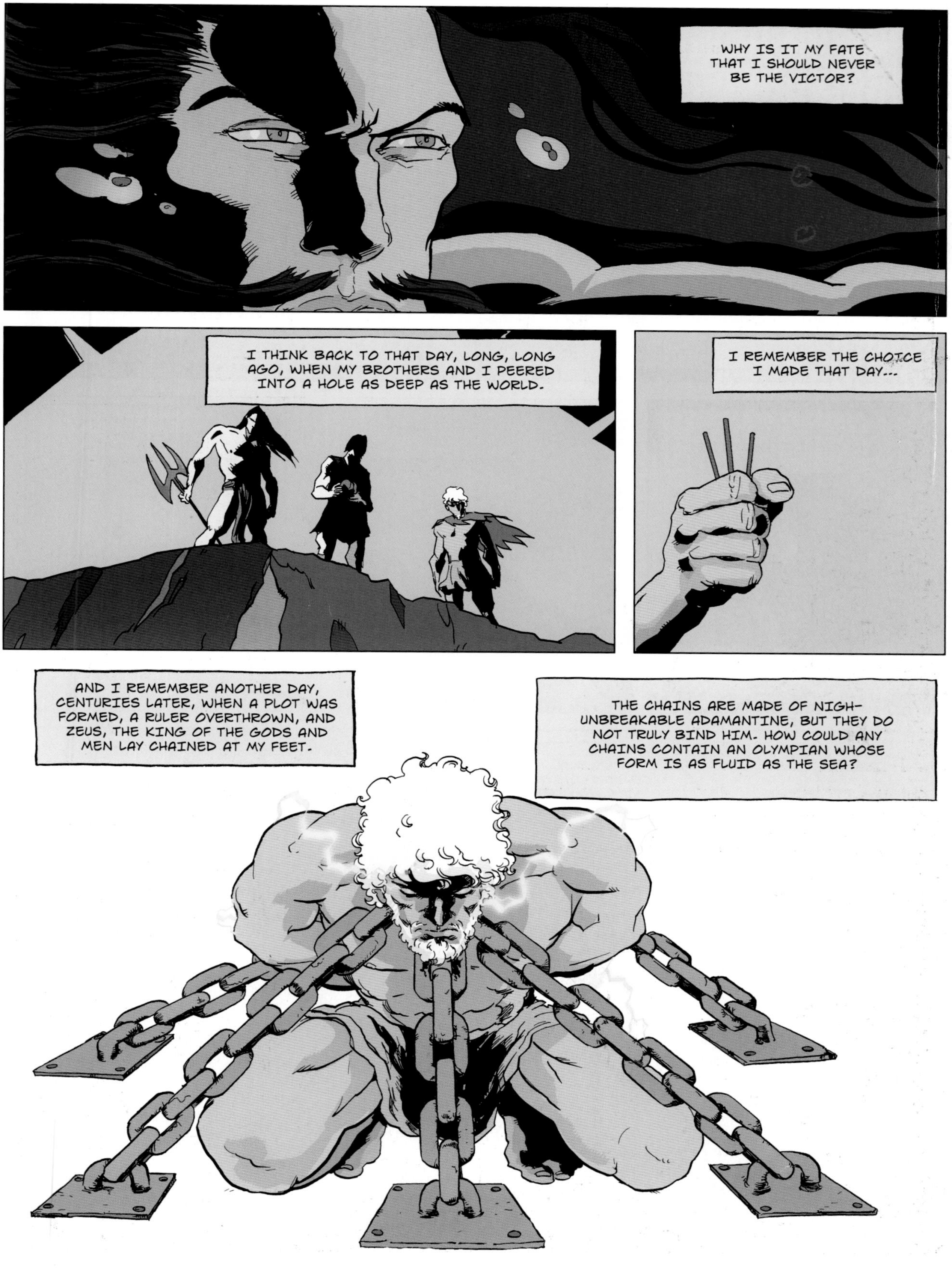
WHY IS IT MY FATE THAT I SHOULD NEVER BE THE VICTOR?
I THINK BACK TO THAT DAY, LONG, LONG AGO, WHEN MY BROTHERS AND I PEERED INTO A HOLE AS DEEP AS THE WORLD.
I REMEMBER THE CHOICE I MADE THAT DAY...
AND I REMEMBER ANOTHER DAY, CENTURIES LATER, WHEN A PLOT WAS FORMED, A RULER OVERTHROWN, AND ZEUS, THE KING OF THE GODS AND MEN LAY CHAINED AT MY FEET.
THE CHAINS ARE MADE OF NIGH-UNBREAKABLE ADAMANTINE, BUT THEY DO NOT TRULY BIND HIM. HOW COULD ANY CHAINS CONTAIN AN OLYMPIAN WHOSE FORM IS AS FLUID AS THE SEA?

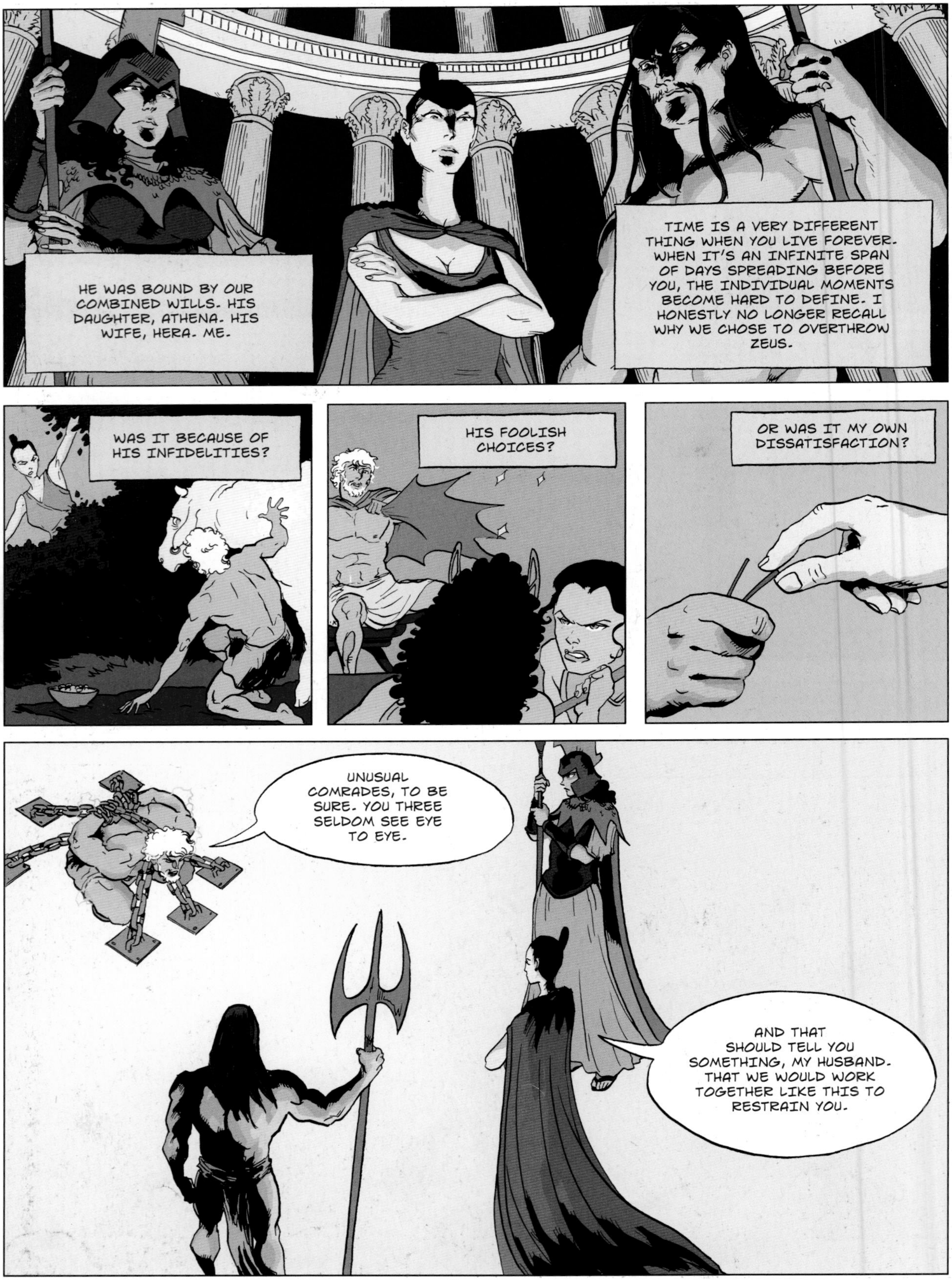

HE WAS BOUND BY OUR COMBINED WILLS. HIS DAUGHTER, ATHENA. HIS WIFE, HERA. ME.
TIME IS A VERY DIFFERENT THING WHEN YOU LIVE FOREVER. WHEN IT'S AN INFINITE SPAN OF DAYS SPREADING BEFORE YOU, THE INDIVIDUAL MOMENTS BECOME HARD TO DEFINE. I HONESTLY NO LONGER RECALL WHY WE CHOSE TO OVERTHROW ZEUS.
WAS IT BECAUSE OF HIS INFIDELITIES?
HIS FOOLISH CHOICES?
OR WAS IT MY OWN DISSATISFACTION?
UNUSUAL COMRADES, TO BE SURE. YOU THREE SELDOM SEE EYE TO EYE.
AND THAT SHOULD TELL YOU SOMETHING, MY HUSBAND. THAT WE WOULD WORK TOGETHER LIKE THIS TO RESTRAIN YOU.

AND YOU SIT THERE, POWERLESS, ALONE.

THAT'S WHAT YOU THINK.

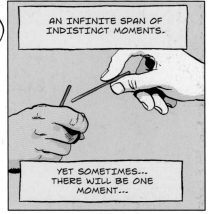

AN INFINITE SPAN OF INDISTINCT MOMENTS.

YET SOMETIMES... THERE WILL BE ONE MOMENT...

THE GROUND, IT TREMBLES—

POSEIDON, IS THIS YOU?

NO. NOT ME—

RKKRUNCH

55

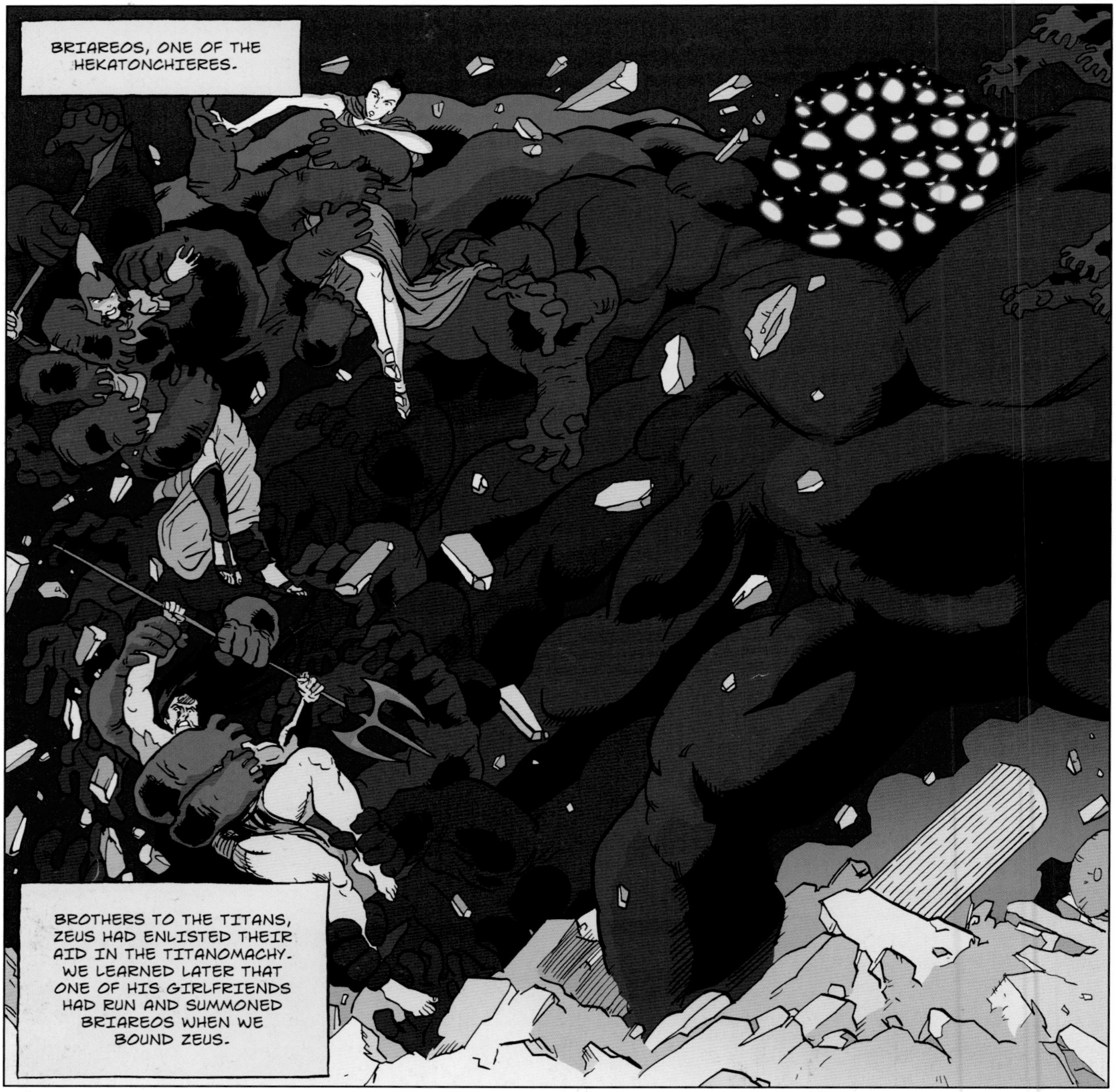
BRIAREOS, ONE OF THE HEKATONCHIERES.
BROTHERS TO THE TITANS, ZEUS HAD ENLISTED THEIR AID IN THE TITANOMACHY. WE LEARNED LATER THAT ONE OF HIS GIRLFRIENDS HAD RUN AND SUMMONED BRIAREOS WHEN WE BOUND ZEUS.

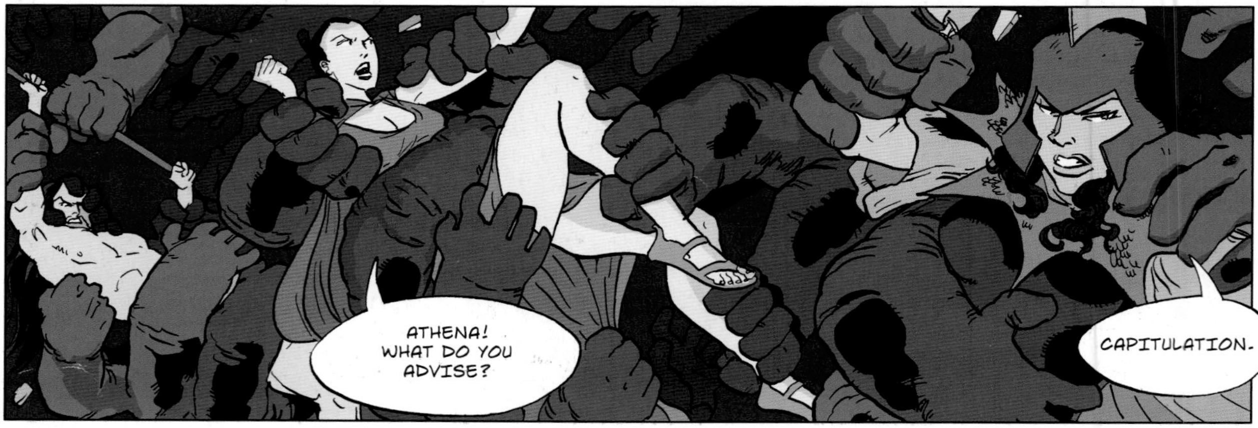
ATHENA! WHAT DO YOU ADVISE?
CAPITULATION.

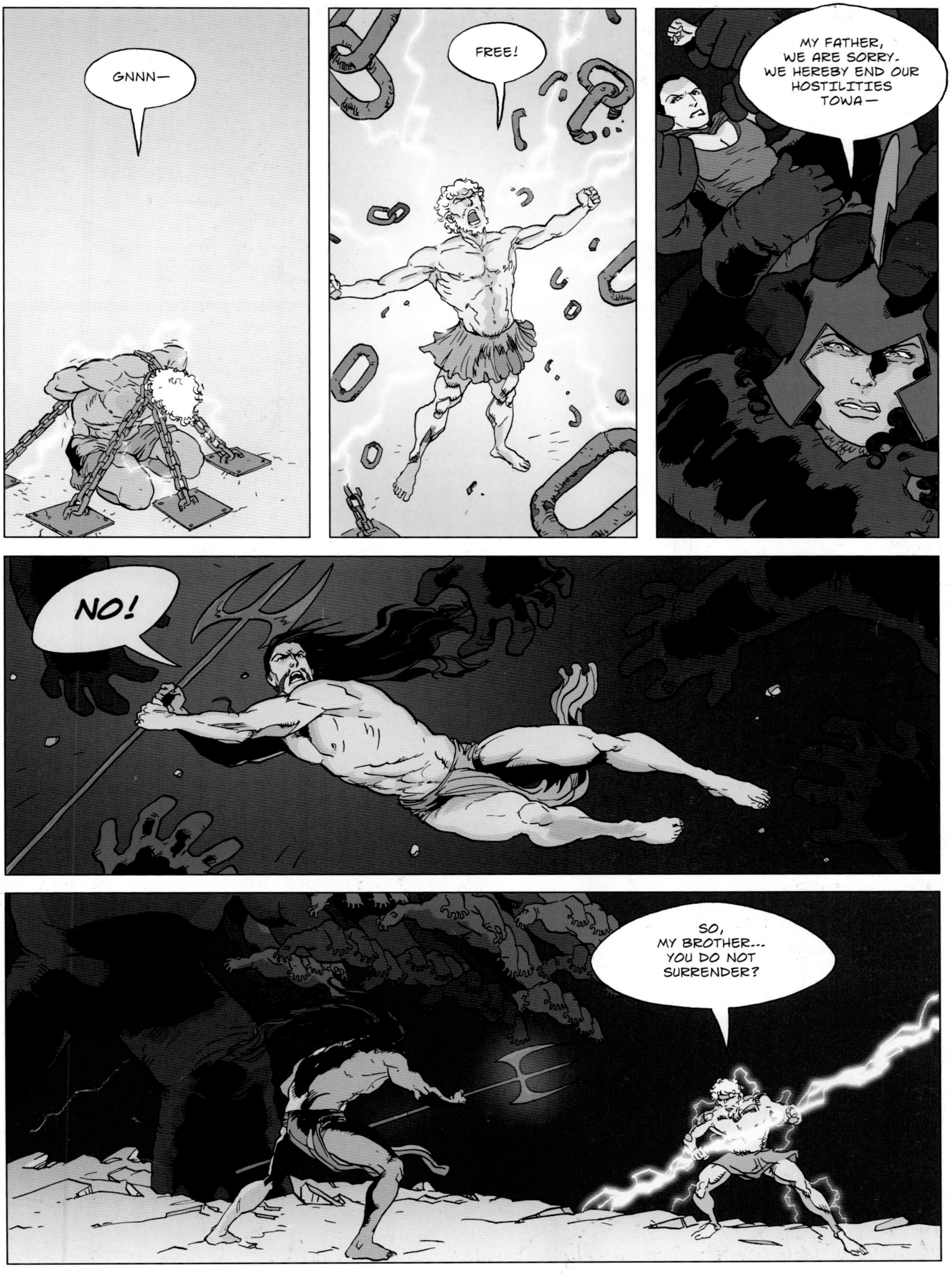
GNNN—
FREE!
MY FATHER, WE ARE SORRY. WE HEREBY END OUR HOSTILITIES TOWA—
NO!
SO, MY BROTHER... YOU DO NOT SURRENDER?

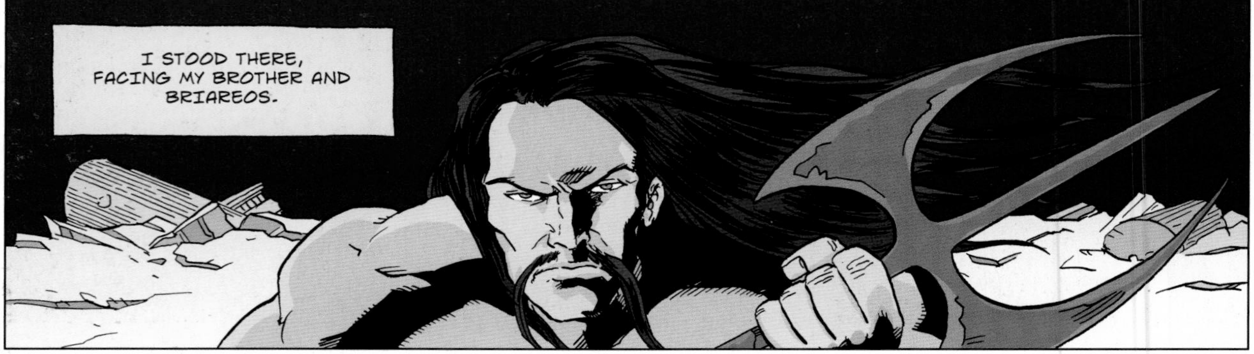
I STOOD THERE, FACING MY BROTHER AND BRIAREOS.

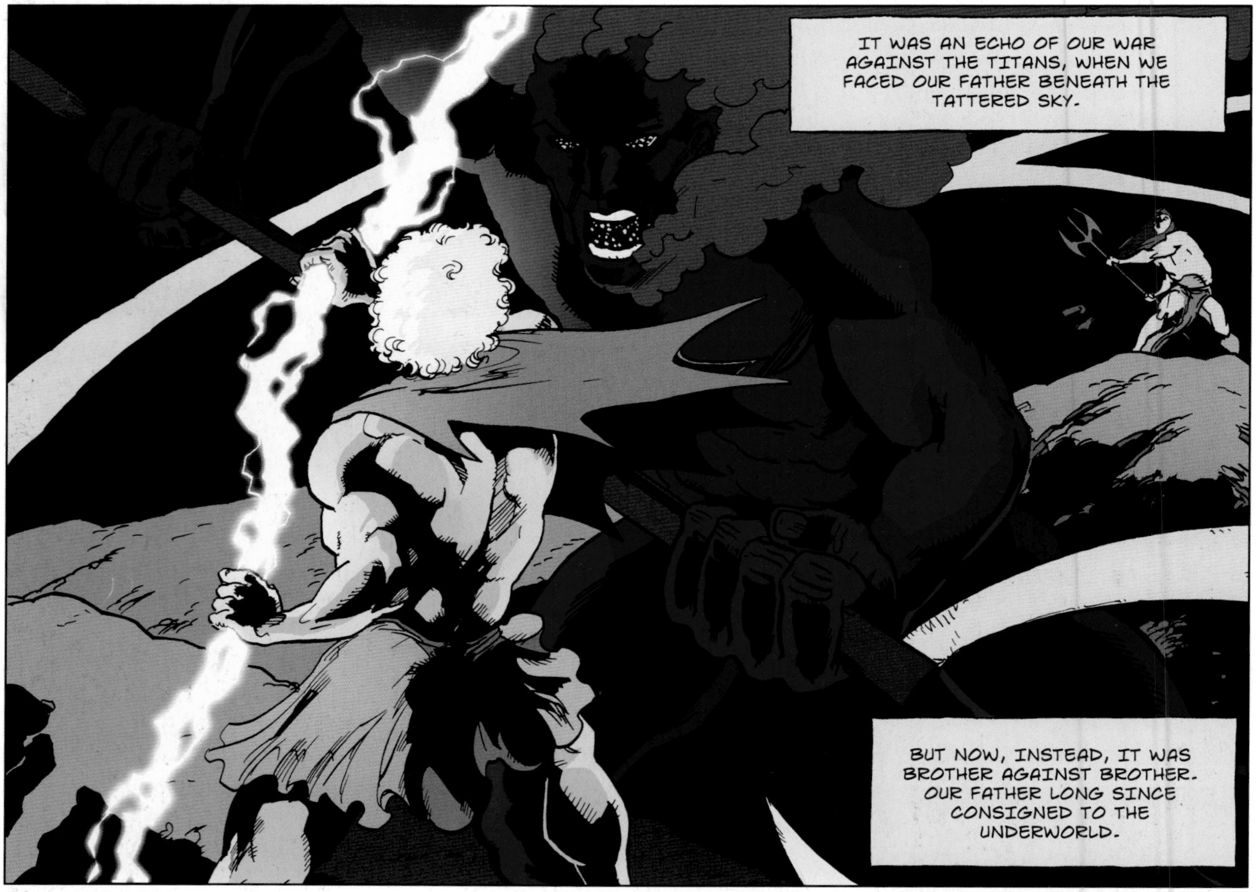
IT WAS AN ECHO OF OUR WAR AGAINST THE TITANS, WHEN WE FACED OUR FATHER BENEATH THE TATTERED SKY.
BUT NOW, INSTEAD, IT WAS BROTHER AGAINST BROTHER. OUR FATHER LONG SINCE CONSIGNED TO THE UNDERWORLD.

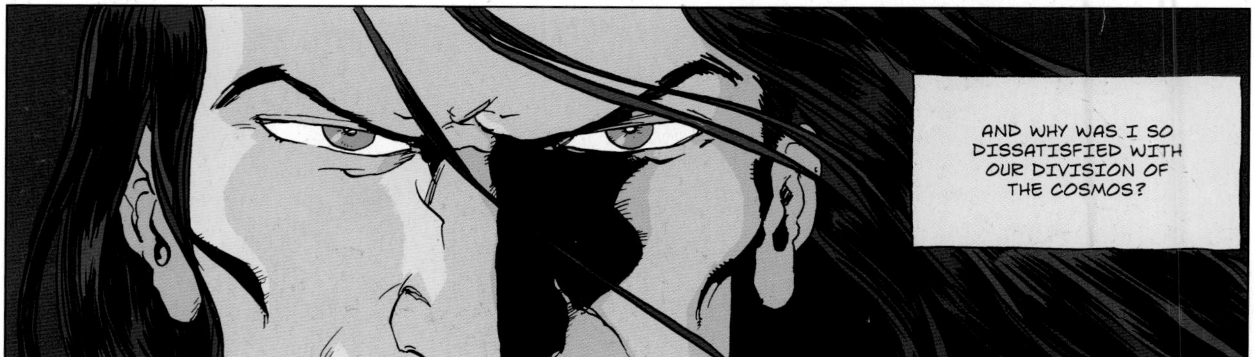
AND WHY WAS I SO DISSATISFIED WITH OUR DIVISION OF THE COSMOS?

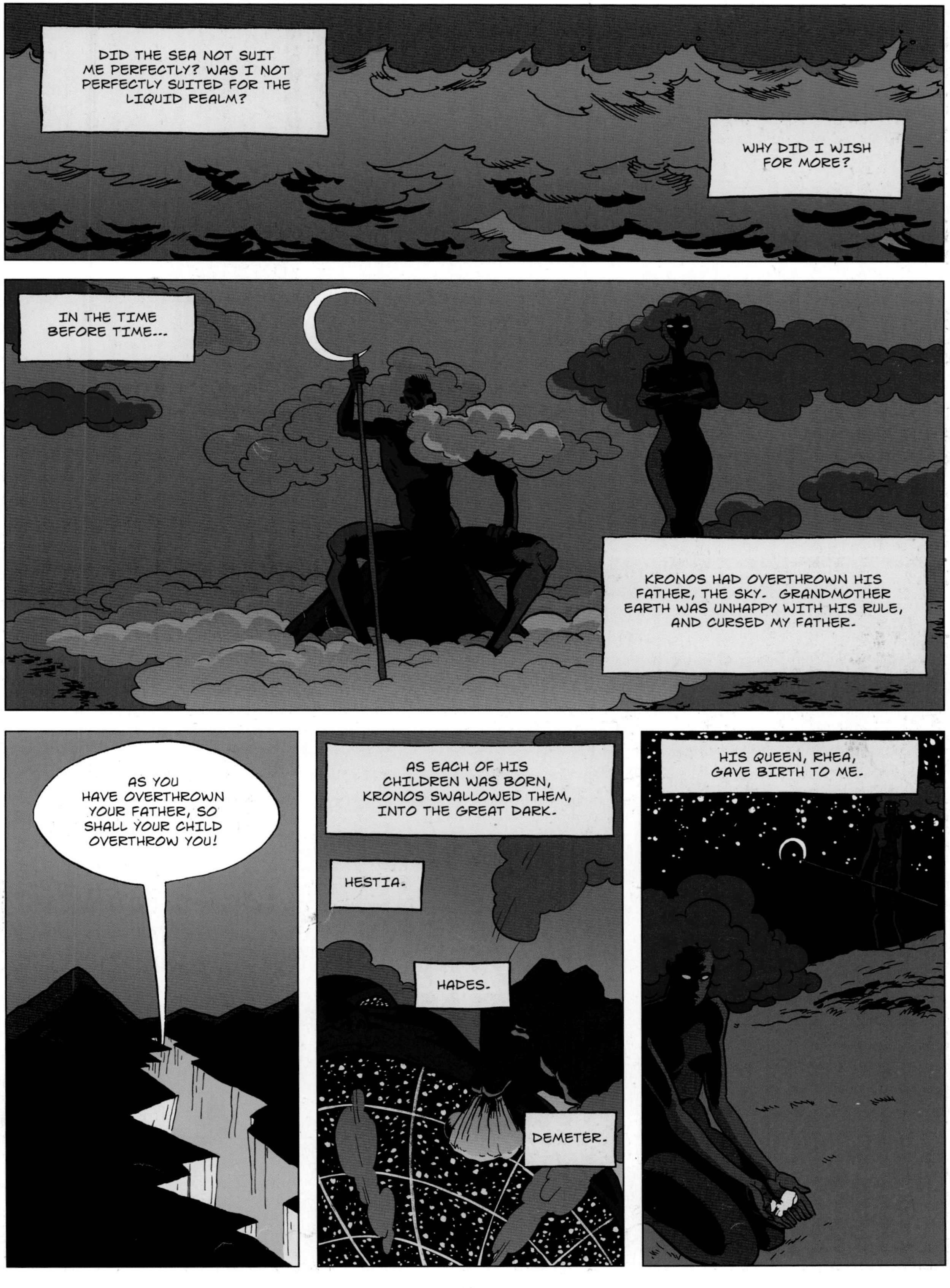
DID THE SEA NOT SUIT ME PERFECTLY? WAS I NOT PERFECTLY SUITED FOR THE LIQUID REALM?
WHY DID I WISH FOR MORE?
IN THE TIME BEFORE TIME...
KRONOS HAD OVERTHROWN HIS FATHER, THE SKY. GRANDMOTHER EARTH WAS UNHAPPY WITH HIS RULE, AND CURSED MY FATHER.
AS YOU HAVE OVERTHROWN YOUR FATHER, SO SHALL YOUR CHILD OVERTHROW YOU!
AS EACH OF HIS CHILDREN WAS BORN, KRONOS SWALLOWED THEM, INTO THE GREAT DARK.
HESTIA.
HADES.
DEMETER.
HIS QUEEN, RHEA, GAVE BIRTH TO ME.

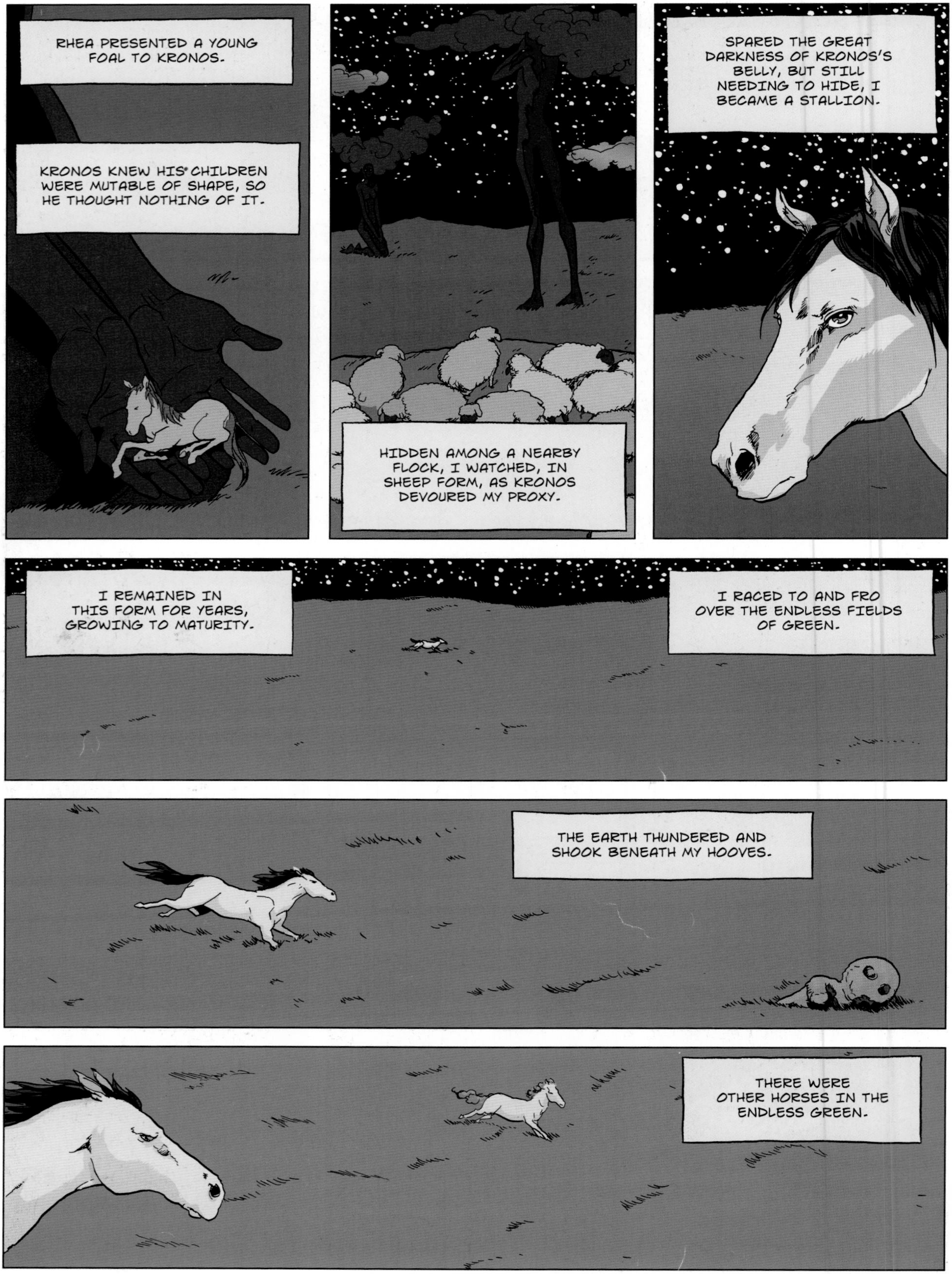
RHEA PRESENTED A YOUNG FOAL TO KRONOS.
KRONOS KNEW HIS CHILDREN WERE MUTABLE OF SHAPE, SO HE THOUGHT NOTHING OF IT.
HIDDEN AMONG A NEARBY FLOCK, I WATCHED, IN SHEEP FORM, AS KRONOS DEVOURED MY PROXY.
SPARED THE GREAT DARKNESS OF KRONOS'S BELLY, BUT STILL NEEDING TO HIDE, I BECAME A STALLION.
I REMAINED IN THIS FORM FOR YEARS, GROWING TO MATURITY.
I RACED TO AND FRO OVER THE ENDLESS FIELDS OF GREEN.
THE EARTH THUNDERED AND SHOOK BENEATH MY HOOVES.
THERE WERE OTHER HORSES IN THE ENDLESS GREEN.

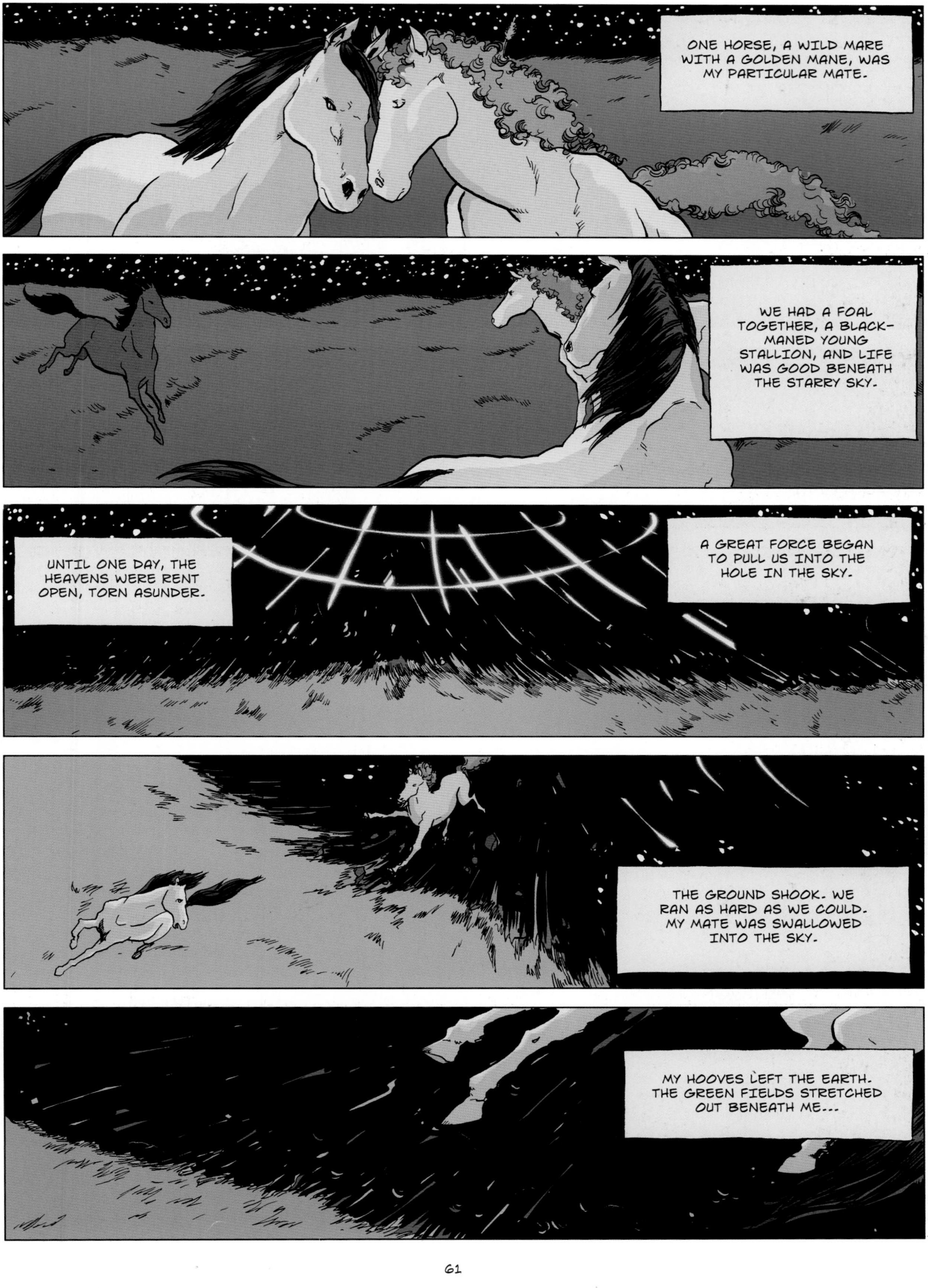
ONE HORSE, A WILD MARE WITH A GOLDEN MANE, WAS MY PARTICULAR MATE.
WE HAD A FOAL TOGETHER, A BLACK-MANED YOUNG STALLION, AND LIFE WAS GOOD BENEATH THE STARRY SKY.
UNTIL ONE DAY, THE HEAVENS WERE RENT OPEN, TORN ASUNDER.
A GREAT FORCE BEGAN TO PULL US INTO THE HOLE IN THE SKY.
THE GROUND SHOOK. WE RAN AS HARD AS WE COULD. MY MATE WAS SWALLOWED INTO THE SKY.
MY HOOVES LEFT THE EARTH. THE GREEN FIELDS STRETCHED OUT BENEATH ME...

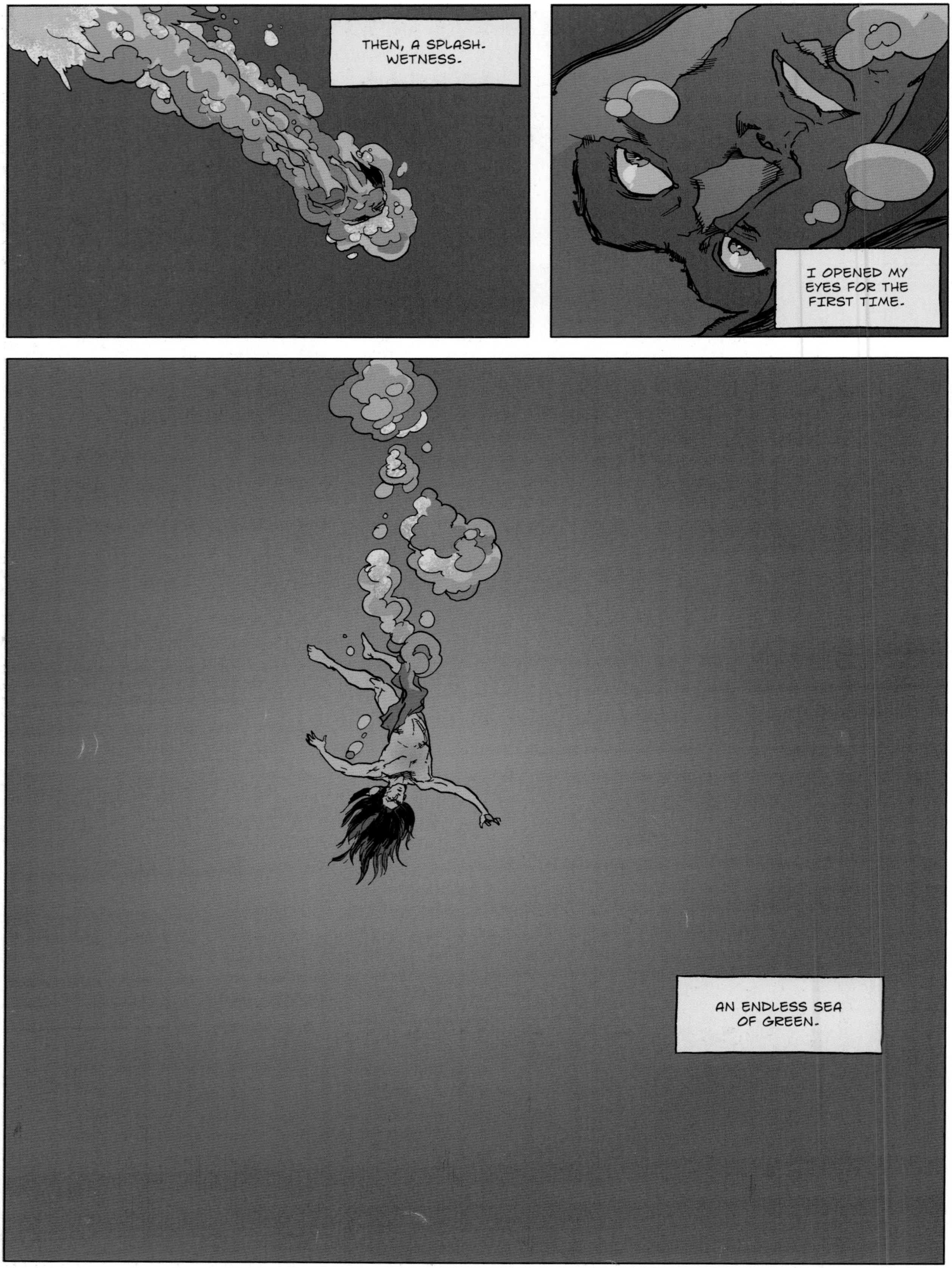
THEN, A SPLASH. WETNESS.
I OPENED MY EYES FOR THE FIRST TIME.
AN ENDLESS SEA OF GREEN.

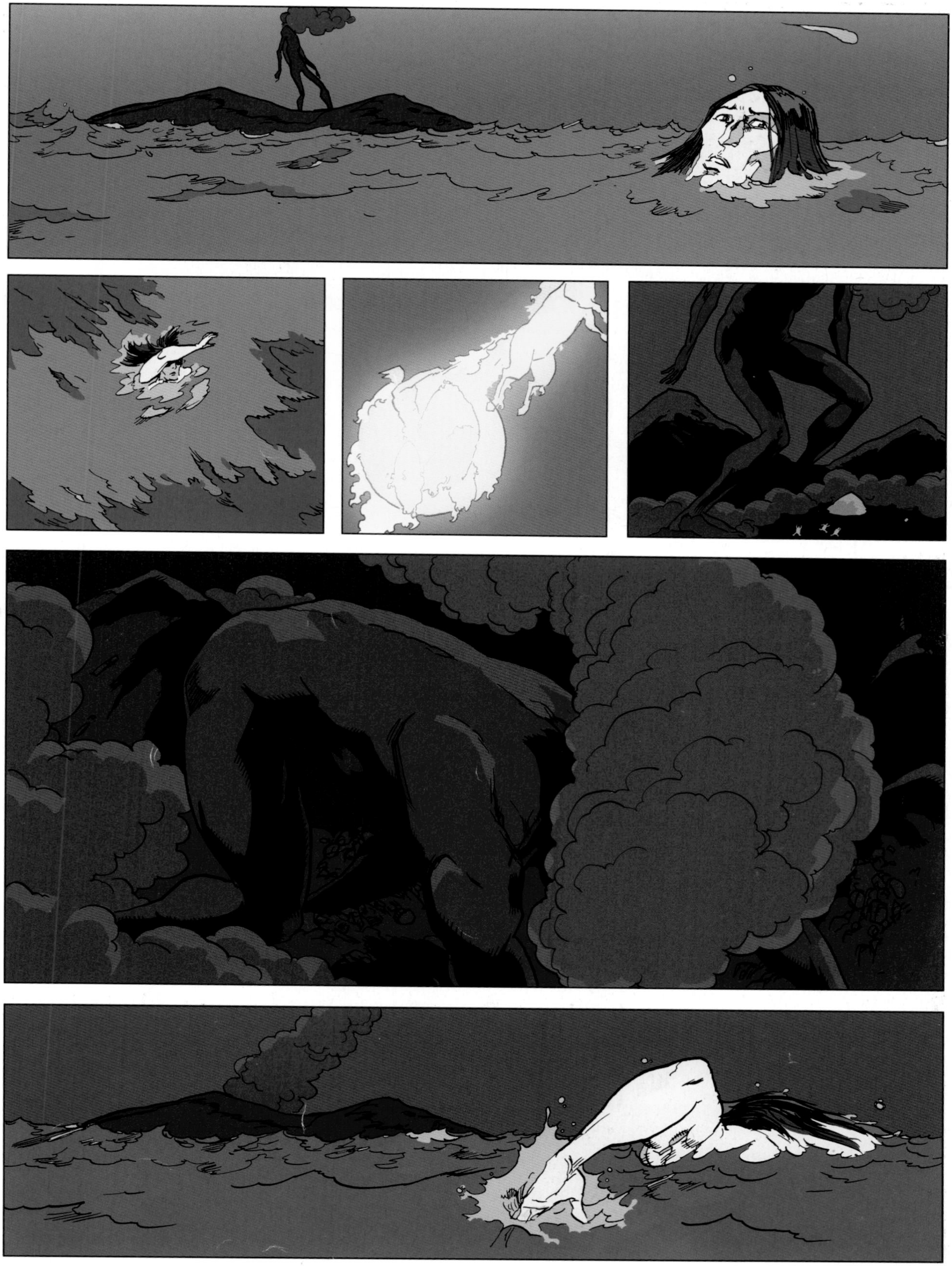

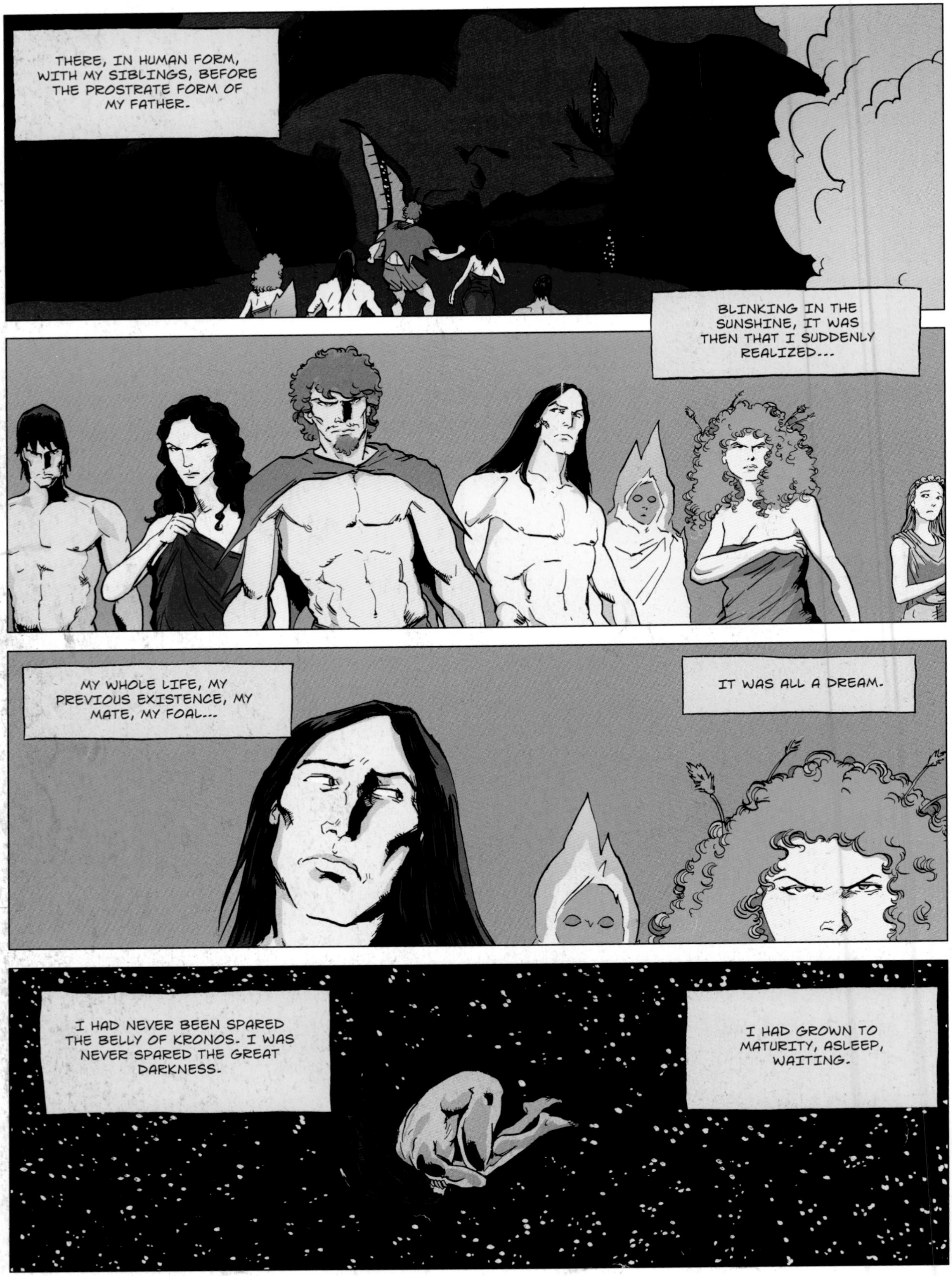
THERE, IN HUMAN FORM, WITH MY SIBLINGS, BEFORE THE PROSTRATE FORM OF MY FATHER.
BLINKING IN THE SUNSHINE, IT WAS THEN THAT I SUDDENLY REALIZED...
MY WHOLE LIFE, MY PREVIOUS EXISTENCE, MY MATE, MY FOAL...
IT WAS ALL A DREAM.
I HAD NEVER BEEN SPARED THE BELLY OF KRONOS. I WAS NEVER SPARED THE GREAT DARKNESS.
I HAD GROWN TO MATURITY, ASLEEP, WAITING.

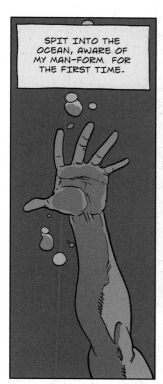

SPIT INTO THE OCEAN, AWARE OF MY MAN-FORM FOR THE FIRST TIME.

AWAKENED INTO A WORLD OF FIRE AND FURY...

CONSTANT STRIFE AND BATTLE, AND THEN, WHEN IT ENDED...

A CHOICE WAS MADE, A SINGLE MOMENT...

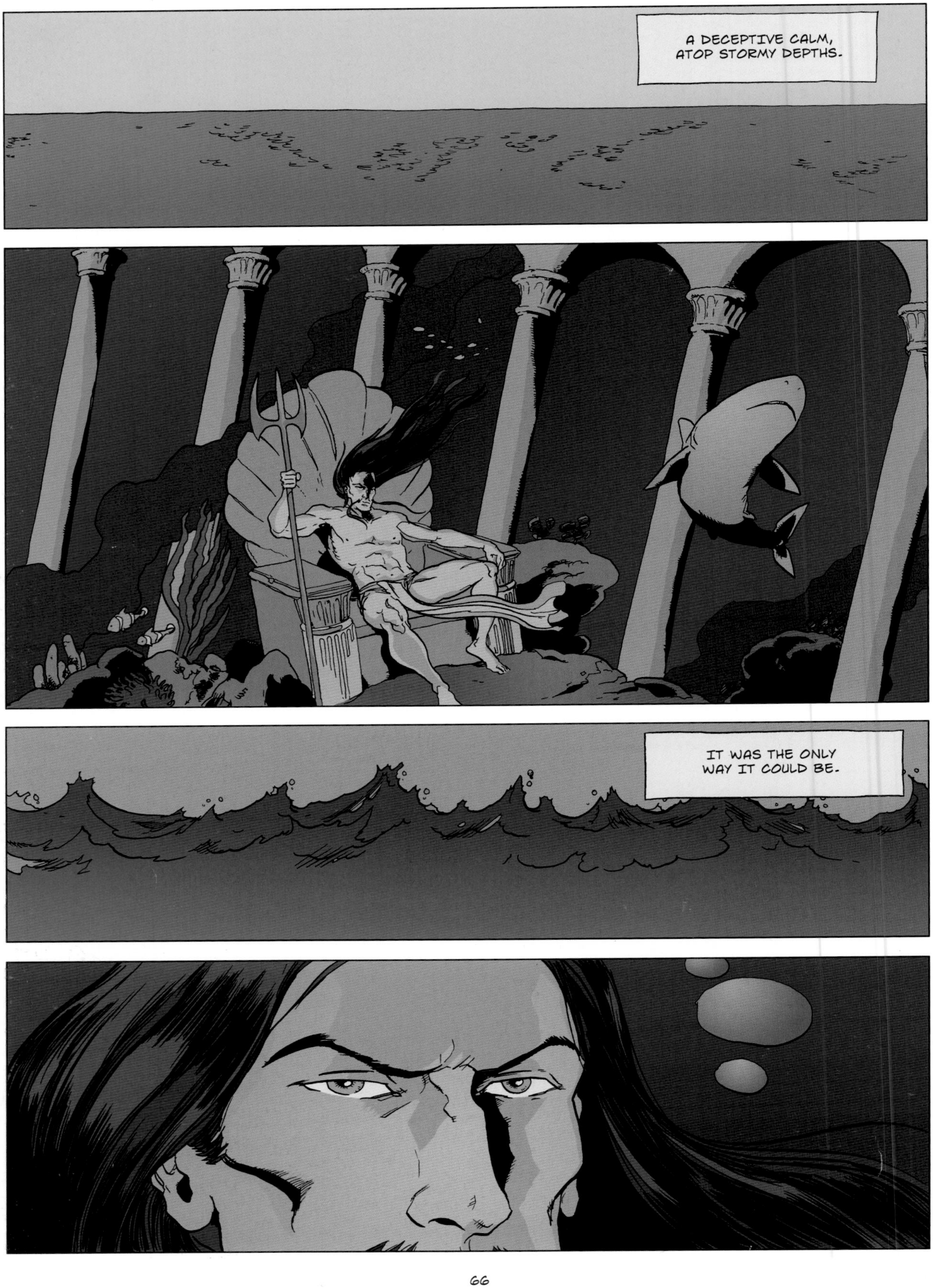
A DECEPTIVE CALM,
ATOP STORMY DEPTHS.
IT WAS THE ONLY
WAY IT COULD BE.

AUTHOR'S NOTE

Whew, this was a rough one.

Poseidon is a hard god to get to know. He appears in many myths, often playing a pretty substantial role, but he's always distant, remote. We mere mortals are not made privy to his desires, his ambitions, his hopes, his fears. He doesn't often let his human side show, so to speak, and humanizing the gods has been part of the mission statement of OLYMPIANS. How best to show the human side of a god like Poseidon?

I had anticipated this problem with the God of the Sea early on and decided, way back when I was first plotting out the whole arc of the OLYMPIANS series, that the best way to deal with the inscrutability of Poseidon was to make him the narrator of his own book. It was a bit of departure—the other books in OLYMPIANS had an omniscient narrator (or three, as in the case of the Fates in ATHENA: GREY-EYED GODDESS) but I figured, what better way to get inside the head of a hard-to-know deity than to have him tell his own story?

So I wrote the book from Poseidon's point of view. And, when I was done with the first draft, I still didn't understand him. Despite the fact that he was the narrator, the book just didn't work; we never got a feeling for the character of Poseidon. He was still hidden from me, as hard to read as the sea.

Back to the drawing board.

I scrapped the whole book. I needed to get to know the character of this very famous, yet very remote god. I couldn't write it from his point of view—I simply did not know him well enough to do that. So then who should tell the story of Poseidon if not him? One day, I had the inspiration—his rival, Athena.

This went much better—writing the book through Athena's eyes, someone I already had a much better understanding of—I was able to capture something of the character of the Earth Shaker. The thing was, eventually I realized that Athena herself maybe didn't have the clearest idea of what made her uncle tick either (if she did, maybe they'd get along better). She had her own ideas, but ultimately, she couldn't know everything. Poseidon is too proud to share his feelings, to show his thoughts. Athena could only know Poseidon through her perception of his actions, and he's a deep, deep guy. Wise as she is, she can only see the surface. But, somehow, in writing out his story through the eyes of another, I suddenly realized how I could write this book successfully in the voice of Poseidon.

Again, back to the drawing board.

with them to the coast their belief in a god of the flowing steppes, of the horses, who was the consort of Demeter.

As a narrator, Poseidon never spells out what he's thinking directly, but I think you can get what makes him tick. He's a middle child, sandwiched between a distant older brother, and a younger brother who gets all the glory. Poseidon narrates his own story to us, the readers, yet he only says one word to another character in the whole book (a defiant "NO," to baby brother Zeus). Never doubting himself, he nonetheless feels keenly that he doesn't belong, and he can't place his finger on why. Like I said, he's a deep guy who may seem like something else on the surface, but there's a lot going on down there that we can only guess at, and the emotions can churn up out of him with ferocious intensity. The book itself mirrors his character—a bit choppy at times, with moments of high, turbulent emotion followed by sudden calm. Expanses of thoughtful serenity are punctuated by abrupt acts of violence.

In short, he's a lot like the sea, which makes a lot of sense. A hard god to get to know, but now, at last, I think I understand him a little better. I hope you do, too.

George O'Connor
Brooklyn, NY
2012

Third time was the charm, I guess. The end result is the book you're holding in your hands right now. The key scene, the one that made it all come together in my mind, was the glimpse into the existence Poseidon dreamed while in Kronos's belly. I included the whole horse sequence to reflect the tradition in parts of Greece that Poseidon, like Zeus, was spared the belly of his father, but it also served as an excellent reason for Poseidon's apparent dissatisfaction with his realm, his allotment. It went some way to explain the apparently incongruous connection between horses and a god of the sea. It spoke to the earlier times, before myth congealed into the form we know now, when the ancestors of the worshippers of Poseidon had never seen the sea, and brought

POSEIDON

EARTH SHAKER

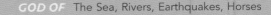

GOD OF	The Sea, Rivers, Earthquakes, Horses
ROMAN NAME	Neptune
SYMBOLS	Trident (his three-pointed spear), Chariot
SACRED ANIMALS	Horse, Dolphin, Bull
SACRED PLANTS	Sea Weed, Ash Tree
SACRED PLACES	The ocean; the Peloponnesian islands; Aegean sea (site of his underwater palace); Athens (site of his fabled contest for sovereignty of the city of Athena); Kos (the island with which Poseidon crushed the Gigante Polybotes)
HEAVENLY BODY	The planet Neptune
MODERN LEGACY	The image of an undersea king with long flowing beard and carrying a trident remains a familiar one to this day, appearing in sources as diverse as *Spongebob Squarepants* and *The Little Mermaid*.

Trident chewing gum takes its name from Poseidon's three pointed spear.

GⱤEEK NOTES

PAGE 1, PANEL 1: The war against the Titans was related in *Olympians Book 1, Zeus: King Of The Gods*.

PAGE 2: Kronos the Titan swallowed each of his children as soon as they were born, in response to a prophecy by Mother Earth that one of his children would overthrow him. Zeus's mother, Rhea, substituted a rock for the baby Zeus for Kronos to eat (Kronos evidently was not very observant) and, sure enough, Zeus grew up to overthrow Kronos. Again, see *Zeus: King Of The Gods* for more info.

PAGE 4, PANEL 2: See *Olympians Book 4, Hades: Lord Of The Dead* for an idea of how Hades felt about his portion of the cosmos. Poseidon's comment "His time hidden from sight made him hard to read" is my little nod to Hades's status as the "Unseen One." This is the first of many (very) little jokes of mine to be thusly spotlighted in this edition of Greek Notes.

PAGE 4, PANEL 4: "He made his home on the tallest mountain left standing"—pretty sure I've had that line in every edition of *Olympians* so far.

PAGES 5-12: The text of these pages is my own translation of the Orphic Hymn to Poseidon. There are a few translations out there, and each of them is radically different from the others, so I kind of cobbled my own version together.

PAGE 9, PANEL 2: Stallions. Poseidon really likes horses. More on this later.

PAGE 13, PANEL 1: Odysseus is the eponymous hero of the famed Greek epic poem *The Odyssey*. Together with *The Iliad*, it's one of the two cornerstones of Western literature. It's crazy good, and you should all read it at some point. This whole sequence with Polyphemos is adapted from *The Odyssey*.

PAGE 16: There is a theory that when the Greeks discovered the giant skulls of woolly mammoths and mastodons they mistook the large socket in the front of the skull (actually for the trunk) to be an eye socket, for one huge, monstrous eye, and that is what lead to the invention of the Cyclopes. As a nod to this, my previous design of the Cyclopes, the immortal brothers of the Titans and Hekatonchieres, as seen in *Zeus*, had thick elephant skin and legs. My design of Polyphemos, a Cyclops of a decidedly different manner, literally has the skull of an elephant, right down to having tusks.

PAGE 17, PANEL 6: The trickle of Acis's blood from beneath the boulder that crushed him, it was believed, gave birth to the river Acis in Sicily. Works for me.

PAGE 18, PANEL 3: "Achaeans" was the name Homer and the Greeks called themselves in *The Odyssey*.

PAGE 19 PANEL 1: There you go, people. The single most violent panel in the entire series of *Olympians*, so far. And it's directly from *The Odyssey!* A book you'll probably end up reading in school! Books are cool, kids!

PAGE 22 PANEL 1: As thorough a warning against drinking, playing with pointy sticks, and eating your houseguests as has ever been committed to paper.

PAGE 26 PANEL 5: The Greek names on the statues that Aegeas is looking at are, left to right, his own and those of his father Pandion, and his grandfather Cecrops. He is no doubt musing on the lack of a statue to follow after his own, and the fate of his royal lineage.

PAGE 28, PANEL 2: If you came here for an explanation of the oracle's prophecy, don't bother—I couldn't understand it either.

PAGE 31, PANEL 2: We derive the name of the ancient Cretan people, the Minoans, from this mythical King Minos. They were the dominant force of the Mediterranean from about the 27th century BCE until about the 15th century BCE. We don't know what they actually called themselves, but it wasn't late for dinner. Haw!

PAGE 31, PANEL 6: More about Daedalus in future volumes of OLYMPIANS.

PAGE 33, PANEL 3: Look! Naked! Point and laugh!

PAGES 38-39: M.C. Escher fans, eat your hearts out.

PAGES 40-41, PANEL 6: My little nod to the famous Minoan fresco of the bull-leapers at Knossos. In ancient Minoa, it was apparently a sport to flip oneself over the horns of a charging bull. Pretty hard core.

PAGE 42 PANEL 5: Poseidon finally gets his Minoan bull sacrifice.

PAGE 43 PANEL 5: Fans of great literature will recognize what Theseus says here as the last line of Jorge Luis Borges's amazing short story "The House of Asterion."

PAGE 43 PANEL 6: The idea of a child Ariadne putting flowers on the Minotaur's horns comes from Patrice Kindl's 2002 novel, Lost in the Labyrinth. A great book, and instrumental in forming my opinion of Theseus as kind of a jerk.

PAGE 44 PANEL 6: See what I said about Theseus being a jerk? Don't worry, we'll see more of Ariadne in a future volume of OLYMPIANS.

PAGE 45, PANEL 6: See? See? What a jerk.

PAGE 46, PANEL 1: Theseus is looking at the statues of the kings of Athens. That's his name on the left there.

PAGE 46, PANEL 4: We previously saw Cecrops as a name on a statue on page 26, panel 5. Cecrops was thought of as half human, half dragon, hence his scaly skin.

PAGE 47, PANELS 3-5: All events shown here were originally depicted in OLYMPIANS BOOK 2, ATHENA: GREY-EYED GODDESS. If you haven't read it already, you oughta.

PAGE 50, PANEL 1: Why indeed?

PAGE 51, PANEL 1: It is, and they are. Athens today is the capital of Greece, and the Acropolis (the temple complex built on the hill, dedicated to Athena) remains one of the preeminent symbols of Western civilization.

PAGE 52, PANEL 5: Look, it's Cetus, the sea monster from OLYMPIANS BOOK 2, ATHENA: GREY-EYED GODDESS. Last time I mention that book, honestly.

PAGE 56, PANEL 1: The Hekatonchieres, the fifty-headed, one hundred-handed brothers of the Cyclopes and Titans. Someone asked me to draw a picture of one of them in his copy of ZEUS, the other day. I just laughed.

PAGE 58: As punishment for his role in the rebellion against Zeus, Poseidon was made to construct the walls of the city of Troy. And that is a tale for another day.

PAGE 60, PANEL 5: Look, it's the stone that Kronos swallowed instead of Zeus as seen in OLYMPIANS BOOK 1, ZEUS: KING OF THE GODS.

PAGE 61: The horse with the golden mane is the goddess Demeter. Their child is Arion, a horse capable of human speech.

PAGE 66: And now you know why Poseidon, a god of the sea, is so obsessed with horses. And why he's so... touchy. Can't say I blame him.

ABOUT THIS BOOK

POSEIDON: EARTH SHAKER is the fifth book in OLYMPIANS, a new graphic novel series from First Second that retells the Greek myths.

FOR DISCUSSION

1 Poseidon, Hades, and Zeus divide up the cosmos by drawing lots. Was this the best way to do this? Was it fair? Was there another way they could have done it?

2 Both Polyphemos and King Minos of Crete are some pretty terrible hosts. Who do you think was worse? I mean, either way, in the end, you're getting eaten by a big hairy monster...

3 As he mentions, a lot of Poseidon's children are monstrous, either in form or in actions. Why do you think that is? What is monstrous about Polyphemos? Or Theseus?

4 In many ways, Poseidon and the other characters are like superheroes. What superheroes can you think of that are similar to characters in Greek mythology?

5 Athena and Poseidon both competed for the city of Athens. Whose gift do you think was better, Athena's or Poseidon's, and why? What do you think Athens would be called today if Poseidon had won the contest?

6 Poseidon doesn't remember why he, Hera, and Athena tried to overthrow Zeus. Why do you think they did it?

7 Why do you think the God of the Sea was also the God of Earthquakes? How about horses?

8 Very few people believe in the Greek gods today. Why do you think it is important that we still learn about them?

THE MINOTAUR

THE BEAST OF THE LABYRINTH

NAME TRANSLATION "The Bull of Minos"

BIRTH NAME Asterion

SACRED PLACES The Labyrinth at Knossos, on the island of Crete

HEAVENLY BODY For such a well-known mythological personage, it could be considered rather surprising that the Minotaur is not more evident in the heavens. He has no constellation, asteroid, or star of his own; the closest he gets is a loose association with the constellation Taurus. However, a series of rockets used to put satellites into orbit are named after Minotaur.

MODERN LEGACY The Minotaur remains one of the most famous of all creatures from Greek mythology, appearing regularly in films, toys, books, and more.

BIBLIOGRAPHY

HOMER, THE ODYSSEY. TRANSLATED BY RICHMOND LATTIMORE. NEW YORK: HARPER PERENNIAL, 1991.
There are many, many, many translations of *The Odyssey;* this just happens to be my own personal choice. Things can change up a bit from translator to translator, so you might find that your preferred version is by someone else. The whole Polyphemos section of this book—one of the adaptations most faithful to the text to appear so far in OLYMPIANS—comes from here.

THEOI GREEK MYTHOLOGY WEB SITE. WWW.THEOI.COM
Without a doubt, the single most valuable resource I came across in this entire venture. At theoi.com, you can find an encyclopedia of various gods and goddesses from Greek mythology, cross referenced with every mention of them they could find in literally hundreds of ancient Greek and Roman texts. Unfortunately, it's not quite complete, and it doesn't seem to be updated anymore.

WWW.THEOI.COM
A subsection of the above site, it's an online archive of hundreds of ancient Greek and Roman texts. Many of these have never been published in the traditional sense, and many are just fragments recovered from ancient papyrus, or recovered text from other authors' quotations of lost epics. It was one of the sources I used for the Orphic Hymn to Poseidon section of the book (pages 5-12), which was very hard to find in an actual book. Invaluable.

MYTH INDEX WEB SITE WWW.MYTHINDEX.COM
Another mythology Web site connected to Theoi.com. While it doesn't have the painstakingly compiled quotations from ancient texts, it does offer some impressive encyclopedic entries on virtually every character to ever pass through a Greek myth. Pretty amazing.

ALSO RECOMMENDED
FOR YOUNGER READERS

D'Aulaires' Book of Greek Myths. Ingri and Edgar Parin D'Aulaire. New York: Doubleday, 1962

The Odyssey: A Graphic Novel. Gareth Hinds, based on the poem by Homer. Somerville, MA: Candlewick Press, 2010

Lost in the Labyrinth. Patrice Kindl. New York: Houghton Mifflin, 2002

Wanderings of Odysseus. Rosemary Sutcliff and Alan Lee. London: Francis Lincoln, 2005

FOR OLDER READERS

Collected Fictions. Jorge Luis Borges. New York: Penguin Group, 1998

The Marriage of Cadmus and Harmony. Robert Calasso. New York: Knopf, 1993

Mythology. Edith Hamilton. New York: Grand Central Publishing, 1999

The Lost Books of the Odyssey. Zachary Mason. New York: Farrar, Strauss and Giroux, 2010

The King Must Die. Mary Renault. New York: Random House, 1988

ODYSSEUS

MAN OF MANY MILES

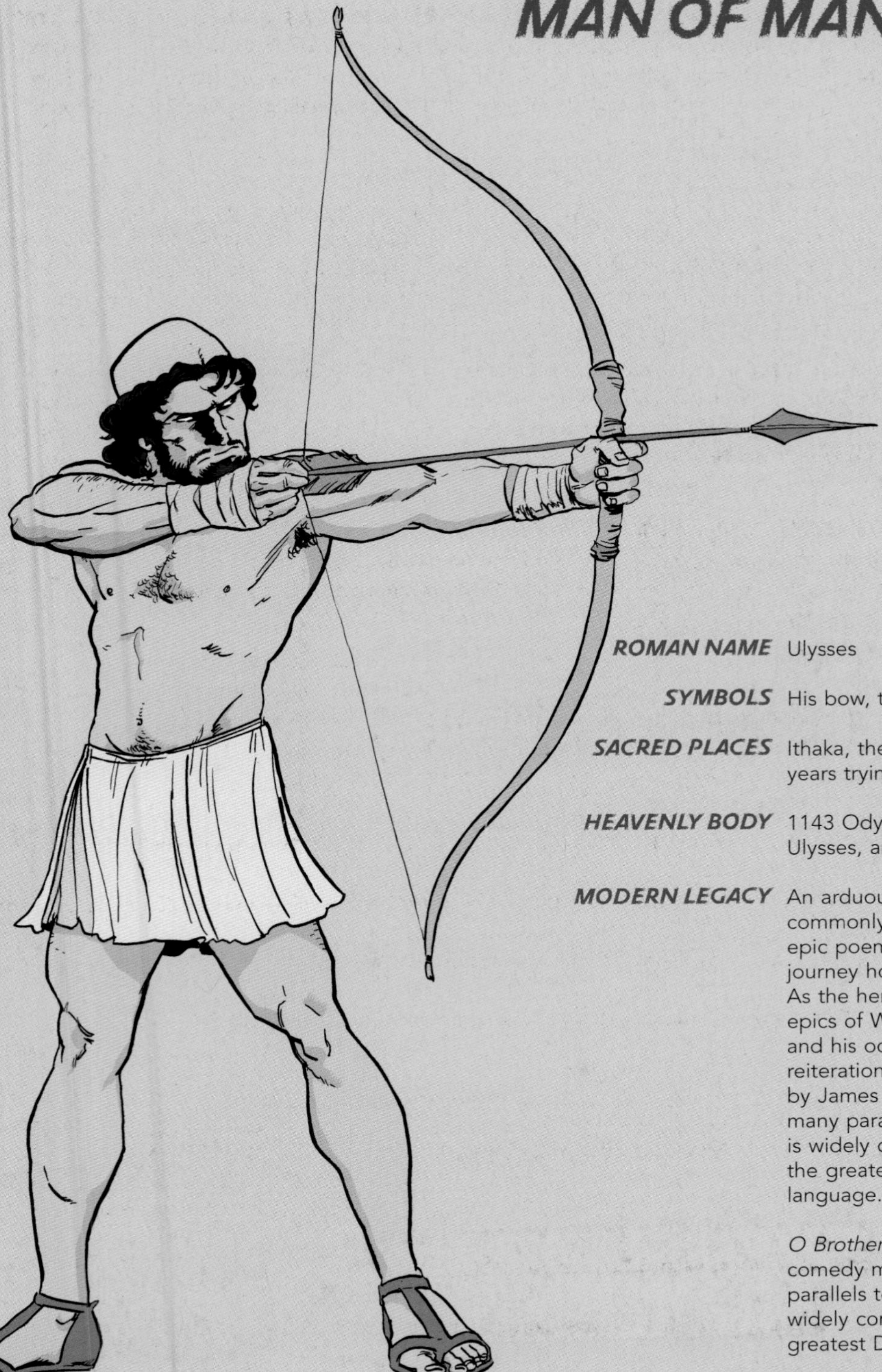

ROMAN NAME	Ulysses
SYMBOLS	His bow, the Trojan Horse
SACRED PLACES	Ithaka, the homeland he spent ten years trying to get back to
HEAVENLY BODY	1143 Odysseus, an asteroid, and 5254 Ulysses, another asteroid
MODERN LEGACY	An arduous trip or journey is still commonly called an odyssey after the epic poem chronicling the ten-year journey home of Odysseus. As the hero of one of the greatest epics of Western literature, Odysseus and his odyssey have had many reiterations through the ages. *Ulysses*, by James Joyce, is a novel containing many parallels to the Odyssey and is widely considered to be one of the greatest books in the English language. *O Brother, Where Art Thou?* is a comedy movie containing many parallels to *The Odyssey*, and is widely considered to be one of the greatest DVDs in my collection.

To the Earth Shaker Himself—I hope we're square now

—G.O.

First Second

New York

Copyright © 2013 by George O'Connor

A Neal Porter Book
Published by First Second
First Second is an imprint of Roaring Brook Press,
a division of Holtzbrinck Publishing Holdings Limited Partnership
175 Fifth Avenue, New York, New York 10010

Cataloging-in-Publication Data is on file at the Library of Congress

Paperback ISBN: 978-1-59643-738-8
Hardcover ISBN: 978-1-59643-828-6

First Second books are available for special promotions and premiums.
For details, contact: Director of Special Markets, Holtzbrinck Publishers.

First Edition 2013

Cover design by Mark Siegel and Colleen AF Venable
Book design by Rob Steen and Danica Novgorodoff

Printed in China by Toppan Leefung Printing Ltd., Dongguan City, Guangdong Province

Hardcover 10 9 8 7 6 5
Paperback 10 9 8